Beyond the Abyss:
Tales of the Supernatural

I0587020

HEATHER SILVIO

Panther Books

Published in the United States by Panther Books, Worldwide.

Correspondence to the author may be sent to:
heather@heathersilvio.com

Visit the author's website here:
https://heathersilvio.com

Cover design by Sonia Freitas at Chloe Belle Arts
https://ChloeBelleArts.com

ISBN (Print) 978-0-9908005-0-7
ISBN (E-book) 978-0-9908005-1-4

The following selections were previously published: "The Chain Unbroken", "Oblivion", "Taking", "Falling", "Nothing", and "War & Death", all in *The Widow of the Orchid*.

To my wonderful husband, Sidney

Also by Heather Silvio

PARANORMAL TALENT AGENCY

Lights, Camera, Action (Episode One)

Reset to One (Episode Two)

That's a Wrap (Episode Three)

NON-SERIES FICTION

Not Quite Famous: A Romantic Comedy of an Actress
on the Edge

Courting Death

NONFICTION

Special Snowflake Syndrome: The Unrecognized Personality
Disorder Destroying the World

Happiness by the Numbers: 9 Steps to Authentic Happiness

Stress Disorders: A Healing Path for PTSD

Contents

The Chain Unbroken

"Damn," Christine muttered to herself, flinging the offending piece of paper away. "What am I going to do?" she asked Fiona, her Siamese, in frustration. The cat looked at her and walked off, leaving Christine to yell after. "A fat lot of help you are!" Christine stood up and trudged over to the liquor cabinet. Opening the door, she reached for a bottle above her head. The squat green bottle with the wide neck was deceptively heavy, lending itself to the assumption it brimmed with an alcoholic beverage. In fact, it held something of a different nature. Pebbles at the base of the bottle gave it its weight.

Christine opened the bottle and withdrew a clump of money. She counted just over one hundred dollars. Christine's rent was due soon, but she hadn't retrieved her secret stash for that reason (as if that would pay her rent!) She had suffered from writer's block the past couple of weeks. Unable to create salable music, Christine resorted to raiding her emergency money supply.

Determined to end her writer's block, Christine collected her money and picked up the flyer on the table. A brand-new keyboard would start the ball rolling, she told herself. Symphonies, top ten hits, all kinds of rhythmic melodies were at her fingertips. The flyer advertised a musical flea market where anything and everything a musician could need or want would be on hand; and below retail value, naturally.

"You want how much for the keyboard?" Christine asked in surprise. She had begun to feel the entire trip was a waste. Unable to find a keyboard for her needs in her price range, Christine had entered the run-down instrument booth in desperation. She went over every piece in the room, it seemed, before she found the perfect keyboard. Fear almost kept her from asking the cost, thus she expressed shock at the quoted price.

"This keyboard is a one-of-a-kind around here," the owner said, staring at her with wide, crazed eyes.

"You don't have to sell me on it," Christine assured him hastily. The man made her nervous, but the deal was too good to pass up. She stared after him as he shuffled to the back to get a box for her. His disheveled appearance and disjointed manner seemed odd. Not wanting to judge,

Christine chalked up the man's presentation to starving artist syndrome.

As the man placed the keyboard in a box, Christine noticed his bruised hands. She startled when images of the man beating a woman to death flashed unbidden before her eyes.

Practically throwing her money at him, Christine grabbed her purchase and raced from the booth. Once outside, nearing her car, she felt foolish. Nothing concrete had happened to make her feel so violently threatened. Why then did she feel relieved to be away from the man and his booth? She shook her head at her behavior and started her car.

Christine was driving up the driveway to her apartment house, humming her last hit, when the voices spoke to her. Not complete sentences, just disconnected phrases that discomfited her. She chalked it up to a delayed reaction to the man who sold her the keyboard. She told herself the voices would go away. They did not.

The voices next spoke while Christine tinkered at her new keyboard. This time the sentence was complete. "We will make all your dreams come true," the voices whispered. "All you have to do," they continued, "is kill someone for us."

Unlike before, Christine's reaction far exceeded mere discomfort. She yelled as though another presence shared the room, then stilled and waited to see what would happen. When nothing did, she dismissed the voices, though not as easily as the first time.

Preparing lunch the next day, she heard the voices again. "Why try to fight us? We can make all your dreams come true. How high is too high a price to pay?" The voices sounded so real, so present, she actually whirled around to look behind her for the source. Nobody stood behind her.

Christine screamed at the voices to leave her alone, but they grew stronger and stronger as each day passed into the next. "They'll go away. They'll go away," Christine chanted to herself, the mantra neither ending the madness nor quieting the voices.

Christine could not sleep. Every time she closed her eyes, visions of mangled, dismembered bodies appeared. And the voices. Voices that refused to grant her even a moment's respite from their incessant chanting.

The insomnia becoming too great, Christine purchased ineffective sleeping pills. Instead of calming her and allowing her to sleep, she saw shadows where none existed, heard noises from invisible sources. All of Christine's nerves were taut. She would snap soon, unless she submitted herself to the voices. She vowed to seek professional help if she couldn't handle the voices herself.

Christine's resolve broke about two weeks after her miraculous flea market find. Having a drink at a local bar one night, Christine invited a man back to her place. Once there, however, her mind filled with the voices' request. A compulsion to kill the man. She felt endangered if she did not. Despite knowing her logic was flawed and fatal, she acted.

"Alex," Christine purred, "would you like a full body massage?" Staring at her, he whispered yes. Christine wrapped her hands around him – then pulled back in fear. "I can't do it," she cried to the voices. Alex got to his feet. "I'm sorry," he said in confusion. "I thought you wanted to." Turning to leave, he never saw what hit him.

Uttering a cry of anguish, Christine hurled a ceramic vase at Alex's head. Had it been just her strength, he might have lived. But the voices filled Christine, screaming in ecstasy, giving her strength beyond human ability. Alex's head imploded with the sound of someone stepping on rotting fruit.

Christine collapsed, sobbing uncontrollably. After a while, she pulled herself together and called the police to report a murder in self-defense. The voices inside her head quieted, content with the night's events.

The police agreed the homicide resulted from self-defense; they'd file no criminal charges. Alex Calden, the "victim", attacked the young lady with intent to commit sexual assault. The attacker pushed the victim close to the counter and she grabbed the vase sitting there. With the element of surprise, she smashed it into the back of his head. If anyone thought to wonder how his head imploded the way it did, what force would have been required, no one mentioned it aloud. It was self-defense. Case closed.

Christine slept well, untroubled by disconcerting visions and dreams. She awoke refreshed, with many new ideas running through her mind. At her keyboard, it was like someone had turned on a faucet. Christine wrote for hours, humming bits and pieces of music, stringing it all together. When at last she stopped, the piece before her was the greatest she had accomplished in her entire life.

Christine called her agent. After humming sections of the new song, she had more than piqued her agent's curiosity. Christine rushed over to present the entire song.

"You are a genius," Ben Dolleg gushed. Representing Christine from the beginning, the agent recognized the promise of the song before him now. Guaranteed top ten hit. "We've just signed a new singer. This song would be perfect for her. We'll definitely use the song."

Christine's eyes lit up, but worry crept in as the agent continued.

"In fact, we've got six more openings on Melissa – that's the new singer – on Melissa's CD. We'll need the songs by the end of the week, though," Ben stated. He smiled, misinterpreting her apprehension. "I have faith in you. Just go wherever you found this piece of magic and get some more. Good luck."

With his words echoing in her mind, Christine drove home frightened and unsure. Today was Wednesday. That left her only two days to write six more extraordinary songs.

"I wrote one fabulous song. I could be satisfied with that and not try to press my luck. No, no, you can write the songs," Christine argued with herself. "I don't know what to do." She made no connection between her wonderful new keyboard and the voices in her head. One couldn't cause the other, could it? Could it?

"You can write the songs. You know what you have to do," the voices whispered to Christine that night as she tossed and turned, unable to fall asleep. She whimpered when the voices returned to their previous strength.

"Please," she cried. "Don't make me do this." But the voices either did not hear her pleas for silence or ignored them. The next day she decided.

"Hi," Christine cheerfully greeted her friend, Gina. "You're the first to arrive. Have a seat, drink a glass of wine. I'll tell you why you're here when the others arrive." Gina smiled at her friend's enthusiasm and accepted the offered wine. Christine must have terrific news to share.

Over the next fifteen minutes, Christine gave similar rehearsed speeches to the other invited guests upon arrival. It was 7:20 P.M. when the last guest took his seat. Christine walked to the fireplace opposite the couches and chairs where Gina, Mike, Kathleen, Jenny, Ken, and Allan sat.

"Welcome," she said. "I've asked you all here to help me celebrate the most important event in my life." She looked at each individual face watching her. These were her best friends, not just random people off the street. *And they dropped all of their previous plans to be here with me*, she thought unhappily. *I need them to create more exquisite music*, she reminded her conscience, which, while not shutting it out, at least dimmed its nagging.

"Yesterday, I agreed to write over half of the songs on an upcoming album," Christine said, glancing out the window over their heads. She seemed anxious for someone celebrating the happiest days of her life. That's when the lights went out.

"Now stay calm everybody," Christine instructed, her own voice eerily calm. "I have candles in the other room. Mike, could you help me, please?" she asked. Mike jumped to his feet to assist. She led him to the kitchen where she rummaged through one of the drawers. Mike started to ask how he could help when Christine turned around.

"I'm sorry Mike," she whispered, and plunged the knife she had taken from the kitchen drawer deep into his chest. He made no sound as she twisted and turned the knife inside of him, feeling the warm blood rush onto her hands. Christine withdrew the knife and, before she could catch him, Mike fell to the floor with a loud thump.

"Everything okay in there?" a voice from the living room asked. "Everything's fine," Christine responded, a funny lilt in her voice. "I bumped the counter." Stepping gingerly over Mike's corpse, Christine reentered the living room. She could dimly see her friends, so she knew they could see her. She hoped they would not see the blood on the knife until it was too late. She did not need a scream to alert the others.

"Where's Mike?" Gina questioned. Christine did not answer, but thrust the knife into Gina's ribcage. Gina twitched and groaned before falling silent and still forever. Christine spun to face her other friends, only to find them gone.

How could she have thought she would get away with this? As if they would allow her to slaughter them? As if they would not see her kneeling before their friend and killing her, the voices and Christine berated themselves, indistinguishable now. She swore under her breath. *They must be somewhere*, she thought. They haven't left. She worried one of the men might have their cell phone, however, and have already called the police. The remaining women were of no concern. Their purses with their cellphones rested beside the furniture in the gloomy room.

A tiny voice of sanity buried deep within her surfaced. "Christine, stop now," it said. "These are your friends. They trusted you." Christine grimaced and shut that voice out. "Not when I'm so close to winning the game." She grinned into the darkness and searched for her prey.

Christine found Ken on the bathroom floor, foaming at the mouth, already dead. Good, she thought in delight. He drank some wine before the lights went out. They all should have been dead by now. The lights had been an unexpected, unpleasant surprise. No matter. Ken was stiff with death. Christine continued the search.

Jenny and Kathleen huddled together on the floor of Christine's closet, praying for rescue. Their prayers went unanswered as the door flew open, revealing them to the madwoman who had been their friend. Christine allowed herself a smile. "Safety in numbers?" she quipped.

Christine entered the room. She plunged the knife into Kathleen, killing her instantly, and used the other hand to rip one of Jenny's eyes free from its socket. Pulling the knife from Kathleen, Christine transferred it to Jenny, already consumed with agony, clutching her ruined eye. Christine closed the closet door and went after her final victim. She knew where he would be.

"Allan, it's no use." Allan spun around in surprise. His back now to the door he had been trying in vain to open, he racked his brain for something, anything that could save his life. He knew she already killed the others. He tried to stall for time while he thought of a way out.

"How did you plan all of this?" Allan asked in desperation, not really interested. Christine took a step forward. At first, he thought she wouldn't respond. She focused her insane eyes upon him.

"It was easy," she said. Her voice sounded triumphant, like she had won some unspoken contest. "I poisoned the wine. Only Gina drank any and apparently not enough to make an impact. I guess I'm no chemist," Christine joked.

"Then the power outage ruined that idea, anyway." Her voice hardened. "It would have been so much simpler if you had all poisoned yourselves." She beamed, an ugly smile that distorted her once beautiful face. "Actually, Ken drank some and helpfully died," she corrected herself. "Since the rest of you didn't cooperate by dying that way, I went with Plan B. Stab all of you."

Allan looked for a way to escape. He saw none and faced his would-be murderer squarely, prepared to battle to the end, wishing he had thought to arm himself with something. Never again would he laugh at the dumb victims in the movies. (Well, obviously, never again, the voices chortled. Could they know his thoughts?) Christine advanced slowly, seeming to hesitate, and he wondered if she was having second thoughts.

"Yes," Christine blurted, almost in response to his thoughts. She smiled wistfully and, for a second, the real Christine shone through – a terrified look in her eyes. Then she vanished, and the hideous murderess returned to finish what she started. The final sound to reach Allan's ears was satisfied laughter, not coming from Christine's mouth, but seemingly from her mind itself.

Christine set about disposing of the bodies in the most efficient manner she could think of. She collected the lifeless bodies into a heap on the floor of her living room. Then she abandoned the task and left the bodies there once her creative juices began to flow.

The flow became a geyser of ideas for her music. It didn't stop until she had six more songs as beautiful as the first, if not surpassing it. She wrote one commercial masterpiece for each life she stole.

The songs complete, Christine called her agent. "Ben, I finished. These songs are amazing. One-of-a-kind," she gushed into the phone. Her nearly palpable excitement infectious, Ben demanded she bring them over at that moment. She obliged, changing from her blood-stained clothes before gathering the sheet music and heading for the recording studio Ben used. The bodies of her dead friends didn't merit a glance as she rushed out the door.

Ben ushered Christine right in upon her arrival. Not easily impressed, her songs shocked him. He stared at her in admiration. She blushed under the scrutiny of his gaze.

"You like them?" Christine asked, the answer evident. As he replied that, yes, indeed, he liked them, Christine clutched at her throat. Ben, who had been leaning on the back legs of his chair, fell to the ground in surprise. He leapt back to his feet.

"Christine, are you all right?" Ben asked, despite the obviousness of her distress. She tried to speak, words struggling to push clear of her throat and mouth.

"I was wrong," Christine managed to speak, her voice little more than a hoarse whisper. "I shouldn't have killed them." She struggled to breathe.

"Killed who?" Ben asked in confusion.

Christine, the real Christine, looked at Ben, tears welling in her eyes. "Allan, Ken, Jenny, Kathleen, Gina, and Mike. Even Alex, I suppose. They were my friends. They trusted me. I left them in my apartment," Christine babbled, her voice still barely above a whisper. Ben picked up the phone, called for an ambulance, and, just in case, reported the possible crime. "I can't fight them," she whispered.

While Ben watched in horror, Christine's face turned faintly blue from asphyxiation. Every time he approached to help, she lashed out and sent him reeling. Christine convulsed and died as Ben looked on helplessly. The police arrived within minutes after Christine's life expired. Another team had found the bodies in her apartment. The deaths of the people in the apartment were obvious. Christine's mysterious passing? The coroner finally concluded Christine had died, in laymen's terms, from an unexplained lack of oxygen to the brain.

Christine had no family to leave her things to, and her will requested every item be sold wherever convenient, with all proceeds going to her listed charities. A week after the sales, a young man in search of an inexpensive, yet high quality, keyboard questioned a woman setting up a booth at a flea market.

"I know that I'm looking for a needle in a haystack. But I really need a new keyboard, and I don't have a lot of money," the young man said almost apologetically to the woman, her blood red fingernails catching his eyes. The woman sized him up and decided to sell him a new keyboard she just received.

"I don't know anything about its last owner, but the keyboard appears to be in excellent condition," the woman explained. "Of course, there is no warranty. And all sales are final. Take a look for yourself." After scrutinizing the keyboard, the man knew he was getting a genuine deal. He paid the low asking price and went merrily on his way, unaware of the trouble he had bought himself.

The woman threw back her head and laughed, a maniacal, crazed laugh – and disappeared forever, the chain unbroken.

Emotional Suffocation

Rivers flow softly in my mind
Unconfined images of life.
Flutes play tenderly to my heart
Storms cut through the love like a knife.

I feel the love overflowing
But not enough to fill the space.
It kills my heart too fast to stop
I need something to take its place.

Who can ease the heavy sorrow?
Can my soul be saved from itself?
The blackness spreads despite the love
My friend, come save me from myself.

Family Time

I survey the room in silence, my heart beating thickly in my chest, the blood pounding in my ears. I stand in my childhood kitchen. My family sits around the table, alternately staring at me, and then at anything but, crying. No, wait. They aren't staring at me. They stare at the TV/VCR next to me. You know, the kind on a tall stand, like the ones offices and schools use. Why would one of those stands be in the kitchen of my childhood? A better question – why am I? I hadn't stood in this room in nearly twenty years. I turn to leave, to head toward the dining room, and it feels like moving underwater. The silence is oppressive and strange, the beating of my heart more a feeling than an actual sound.

Unexplainable fear blossoms in my body as I stare at the

scene unfolding in the dining room. My family, again, only different. I stare at the faces, one by one, trying to make sense of what I see, trying to calm the irrational fear coursing through me. Softly illuminated by the flickering candles on two birthday cakes, the people sitting around the dining room table are indeed my family. From twenty years ago. They watch a spot below my face and to the right, looks of identical happy expectation on their faces while they sing. I cannot hear them, though I can make out the words. I have stumbled into a birthday party. Why am I so afraid?

I turn again, trying to head toward the bedrooms down the hallway, past the living room. The feeling of being underwater intensifies and I struggle for breath. I gasp, words trying to form in my throat, trying to come out of my mouth, but nothing happens. Finally, air pushes through me, and I find my voice.

"Mom!" I scream the word and then the world becomes silent, with only that strange feeling of my heartbeat in my ears.

Nothing. Nobody comes running. The silence remains as if I had not spoken at all. I realize I also have not moved toward those back bedrooms, but still stand at the head of the dining room table, surrounded by happy partygoers.

Unrelenting fear at the core of my being increases at an alarming rate. Somehow, I know I must figure out what is going on before I die. I stare at each of the faces around the table. My father, still singing "Happy Birthday." How long is that damn song, anyway? My eyes shift to the woman seated to his right. Kind eyes in a middle-aged face. My aunt, looking 25 years younger than I knew her to be. To her right, one of my brothers, watching everyone sing. A lighted birthday cake before him. Seven candles on the cake tell me I am ten years old in this little... fantasy. To the birthday boy's right, our older brother, recently (in this tableau) turned thirteen. Next to him... our mother. Mom's lips move like the others, but her eyes are not smiling and carefree like the others.

I frown, trying to read my mother's lips. Then I realize she is peering straight at me, and not where everyone else is looking. I focus on the words my mother mouths to me.

"Come back."

Just those two words, over and over, as I remain paralyzed with fear. What is going on? The fear suffocates more than the silence.

Turning in the strange atmosphere, I return to the scene in the kitchen. The tableau morphs into my family in the present, but still sitting around my childhood kitchen table. A couple of them weep, some try not to. Mom, Dad, brothers, aunt.

Where am I in this picture?

I face the television to my left. That's when I see the man in a business suit standing on the other side of the television. He stands stiffly, uncomfortable, as if he does not like the business at hand. He watches my family watching the screen.

I move to view the screen.

The fear that had subsided as I contemplated these bizarre scenes slams back, growing to the point where I feel certain the anxiety will kill me. Right this second.

On the television screen, a young woman walks along a darkened street. She glances up to note the broken streetlight that would have provided light. Thankfully, a full moon prevents pervasive darkness. She is not afraid, even though she is a young woman walking alone down a darkened street. She is familiar with this route. She is going home. Returning from school, from the market, could be anything. The strap of her bag, showing she has, in fact, come from school, rests on her right shoulder, so that she bends ever-so-slightly in that direction. She is carefree, walking home alone from college on a darkened city street.

I know that scene, know that young woman. That is me, walking home, as I had done so many times before.

The men come from nowhere, birthed from the shadows around the young woman. At first, her awareness of them remains incomplete, as she thinks ahead to her evening at home, deciding what homework, if any, she'll do that night.

Then she is pulled into the moment when the four men encircle her. In the dark, it is difficult to tell if they are white, Latino, or light-skinned black men. In the end, it is irrelevant anyway. With an unexpected punch, the young woman slumps to the ground. One of the men takes her bag while yet another pulls her up by an arm.

I struggle to breathe again, watching the scene unfold. I realize all of my fear is for the young woman in the video. I don't stop to wonder how someone took such a video in the first place. Such information does not matter. I do not remember an attack like that. But I know all of my fear, the suffocating atmosphere, the silence, all come from the woman in the video. It all comes from myself as I am brutally assaulted, with my family bearing witness.

My breath has grown shallow. The fear diminishes and my heartbeat slows. I feel light-headed and the room shifts and moves. I am dying.

Images on the screen become indistinct. I see myself on the screen in a hospital bed, watch the doctors quit moving frantically, watch the machine above my bruised and battered face go to flat-line. The room darkens as the picture on the screen fades.

This is your life, I have time to think. Or death, to be accurate.

I glance one final time at my family around the table. In the growing darkness, I can still discern faces. Aunt, brothers, father, and mother. Mom looks right at me, not at the screen or at her lap, unlike the rest of my family. She speaks to me.

"Wake up!" Those two words, over and over again.

Near absolute darkness surrounds me. I no longer hear my heart beating thickly in my chest, or feel the blood pulsing in my head. There is almost nothing.

I don't want to go. I am not ready to leave yet. No matter what those men have done, I will mend. That strong and carefree young woman exists within me. I am loved.

The room brightens and I hear a mechanical beep on the screen that matches the beat in my chest. All the faces, save one, stare hopefully at the screen. My mother still stares at me, mouthing those words, "wake up", but now she looks satisfied, knowing I had heard her message. As the room comes into focus, my heartbeat grows until it pounds, accompanying the most incredible pain I have ever felt.

I wake up screaming.

Oblivion

Twirling, spinning, into oblivion
where existence is not reality.
No fear and no pain,
but hopes and dreams die.
No love, no life, no vitality.

Oblivion is a hollow place
where thunderous storms rage forever.
Hellish damnation,
with nowhere to run.
There is no escape, now or ever.

Screams of horror surround you.
Oblivion is but a nightmare.
Not one you can return from at will,
Dwell inside it forever,
If you dare.

The Experiment

The man stepped out his front door into a large open field. Nothing but rolling hills surrounded him. The sky darkened and evil shrieks filled the air. Large, prehistoric shapes loomed in the hidden distance. Out of the sky swept birds resembling pterodactyls, crying out in hunger. One bird dove toward the man's head, its talons hooking in the tender flesh of his neck, piercing his jugular vein. His life blood, warm and moist, flowed out...

"That's it. I woke up after that, Dr. Pine," the man said with a sigh.

"That's quite an interesting dream you had. What do you think prompted it?" the psychiatrist probed his patient.

Andrew Mandley glanced apprehensively at the doctor. "I'm not sure where it came from, but it's rather obvious what caused it." He raked his fingers through his blond hair in a classic show of nerves that Dr. Pine did not miss.

"What is so obvious?"

Andrew's blue eyes darkened to near-obsidian in color. "My disease, what else?"

"Agoraphobia is not a disease the way you are making it out to be – and you know that," Dr. Pine admonished in a gentle tone.

"I know that, Doctor, but when I can't even take my daughter to the park, it feels like a terminal illness," Andrew moaned.

Buzz. Dr. Pine reached over and turned off the alarm. "That's all the time we have. We'll discuss your dream further next week. I'll see you then." He stood.

Andrew followed suit, extending his hand.

Dr. Pine gripped his patient's hand and beamed. "Don't worry. We're making progress."

Andrew merely nodded and approached his front door, stopping a distance away. "Sorry I can't show you out," he apologized, again.

"You say that every time I leave. It's okay," the doctor assured Andrew, again. Dr. Pine walked the rest of the way to the door and let himself out.

Andrew marveled at how self-assured the man appeared about everything. Perfectly combed salt and pepper hair, fashionable new suit, a true doctor. Andrew walked back to his couch and collapsed into the comfortable material.

Agoraphobia. It sounded more like a fatal disease than a psychological illness, no matter what the good doctor said to the contrary. Until he could control his fears, Andrew knew he would remain trapped inside his own home. He sighed and closed his eyes. A small hand tapped him on the shoulder. He pretended not to notice.

"Daddy," a voice said. He smiled, despite himself. Tinkling girlish laughter rewarded him. He could feel the strain of the session floating away. "Daddy, it's not bedtime, yet. It's dinnertime. Mommy says dinner is all ready. C'mon Daddy, get up."

Andrew enjoyed listening to the pleasant little voice. He yawned as wide and as long as he could. Then he stood up, pretending to notice his daughter for the first time.

"Hello, honey. How's my birthday girl?" He picked her up, groaning from her weight.

"I don't weigh that much, Daddy. Even though I turned six today," she informed him.

"You're getting old. You better slow down or soon you'll be my age. Thirty," he teased her.

A voice from another room called out. "Michelle, you tell your daddy he's thirty-five."

Andrew carried his daughter into the kitchen and set her down on a counter. He crept up behind his wife. He loved her as much today as the day they married, with her curly brown hair, laughing blue eyes, and wide smile with the crooked bottom teeth. Damn, he sounded sentimental.

"You know, you're thirty-four. Almost as old as I am, Pamela."

She laughed and elbowed him gently in the ribs.

"Maybe so, but you'll always be the old man in the house. And you should know better than to ever say a woman's age aloud!" She and Michelle laughed at Andrew's stricken expression. "Don't worry, though. Shelly and I will love you even when you're old and gray. But not if you get yellow teeth," Pamela warned. The family chuckled at the image of Andrew, old and gray with yellow teeth.

"That's enough picking on me. Let's eat."

* * * * *

Racing engines and wailing sirens cried out in the night. A nondescript car screeched to a stop outside the two-story brick house, ruining the serenity of the night. Detectives went to the front door, but never had a chance to knock, for the door flew open. Standing before them was a man facing perhaps the greatest shock of his life.

"Please, you must find her, you…" The man staggered back away from the door, face pale. He turned and walked hastily away, calling to the police detectives over his retreating shoulder. "I'm sorry. Please come in." He cursed himself for being so feeble.

The detectives entered the house, following the man as he headed for what appeared to be the kitchen. Reaching his hurriedly approached destination, the man turned back, apologetic for his behavior.

"Sorry. That must have seemed odd, my running away after calling you here," he spoke in a rapid jumble. "I wasn't trying to be rude, really. I, um, have a strong fear of the outdoors. Agoraphobia? Do you know it? Please sit down and I'll tell you what has happened. Or at least what little I know," the man murmured.

One detective removed a notebook from his front pocket and flipped it open. "Andrew Mandley? I'm Detective Palmer and this is Detective Harrison. The 911 report states that you called in what you believe to be your wife's kidnapping," the officer began. "What makes you believe your wife has been kidnapped?"

Andrew hesitated before answering. "Well, you see... Pam's missing, but—"

Detective Harrison cut him off. "How long has your wife been missing?"

"About an hour, but—"

"An hour?" Harrison responded in disbelief, his green eyes narrowing in annoyance. "With all due respect, your wife could have gone to run an errand."

"In the middle of the night? No, I don't think she left of her own free will," Andrew explained. "There's blood..." His voice trailed off as an involuntary shudder wracked his body.

Palmer glanced up from his notebook in surprise so fast

it knocked curls of black hair into his brown eyes. "Blood? You didn't mention that to the dispatcher." He scanned the report again, knowing there would be no mention of blood.

"No? I didn't mention it, I guess. I was – am – confused and worried. The trail runs from the bedroom to the living room, then disappears," Andrew described, pointing vaguely off to his side.

Harrison spoke in a softer tone. "Show us the blood, please. Have you touched or otherwise disturbed anything in the house?" he asked.

A crash from upstairs interrupted Andrew's negative answer. Both detectives started for the base of the steps. "Is anybody else home?" Harrison inquired, pausing for a moment, his red hair glowing from the reflection of the hall light above his head.

"Yes," Andrew answered.

"Who?" Harrison's patience was running thin.

"My daughter, Michelle. I checked on her before calling you and she was sound asleep." Andrew looked around the room distractedly, as if searching for something he knew would not appear. Detective Palmer, meanwhile, was already half-way up the stairs and speaking to the little girl who stood at the top. With her blond hair and bright blue eyes, she resembled a living doll.

"What's going on?" Michelle asked, yawning. "I knocked over the lamp in my bedroom," she apologized.

"That's okay," Palmer assured her. "Would you please come downstairs with me? I would very much like to talk to you." The girl regarded his offer with suspicion.

"Where's my Daddy?" she asked instead.

"He's downstairs with my partner. Please come down and talk with us. Your Daddy will be there." Palmer grinned.

"Okay," the girl consented grudgingly.

Andrew rushed over and hugged Michelle after she walked into the kitchen. "Are you okay?" he asked her. "We heard a crash."

"It was my lamp," she told him. "I knocked it over."

"Why were you getting up?" Harrison asked.

"I was thirsty," Michelle snapped.

"Is this your daughter?" Palmer interrupted.

Andrew released his daughter. "Yes, this is my daughter, Michelle. Honey, say hello to the nice detectives. This is Detective Palmer and this is Detective Harrison," he pointed out each of the detectives.

Michelle stared at Harrison. "Do people call you Carrot-top?"

"No." Harrison had never liked kids. He might have looked like a jolly fat cop, but he and kids had never mixed. Palmer chuckled at the question. He was short and wiry and usually got the nicknames. In fact, some of their more 'literary' fellow detectives called the partners Mutt and Jeff.

Michelle whispered hello to the detectives. "Has something bad happened?" She glanced from face to face.

Andrew sat down at the table and took his daughter's hands in his. "Yes, sweetheart. Your mother is missing." Michelle didn't seem affected by this news.

Harrison noted Michelle's odd reaction to the news about her mother. Not only did she not seem upset, she didn't seem surprised. She merely looked at her father, who didn't think anything was abnormal about his child's lack of emotion.

As if realizing her behavior was inappropriate, Michelle began crying and flung herself into her father's arms. After a few moments, she disentangled herself and asked to be excused. Her eyes were bone dry. Harrison's brow furrowed at this display. After Michelle went upstairs to bed, Harrison repeated his request to see the blood. Andrew nodded and led them to his bedroom.

The master bedroom was at the back of the house on the first floor. Blood ran from there up the main hallway to the living room right off the foyer. The detectives had not seen the blood when they had first entered the home. This time they saw the trail; a small amount of blood, but enough to suggest something had occurred there.

In the bedroom, there was no expected pool of blood. A trail started at the foot of the bed and continued out the door. Same in the living room. The blood trail stopped in the middle of the room as if the source had vanished.

* * * * *

"Are you honestly trying to tell me you have no idea what's going on?" The irate and incredulous voice of the head of the Federal Bureau of Investigation thundered over the phone line.

"That's exactly what I'm telling you. We have nothing to do with the disappearances. Why would we take our own citizens? And in such numbers?" the head of the Department of Homeland Security scoffed in response.

"Gee, I don't know. Perhaps because people who operate above the law sometimes forget who they're supposed to be protecting!"

When the phone went silent, the head of the Department of Homeland Security sighed. *If you only knew*, he thought, before picking up the phone.

* * * * *

"Who's there?" the solitary woman called out to her unwanted visitor. A shape approached the bed in the darkened bedroom. "Please... take whatever you want. There's money in the—" Silence as a flash of light engulfed the woman. The empty room smelled of copper, emanating from the bloody trail on the floor.

The night was alive with faint voices speaking in fear, and the silence of a town vanishing. Over three days, one half of the citizens of Haweia Cove (population 3000 – A great place to raise your kids!) disappeared.

* * * * *

"Great. We have 1500 disappearances that make no sense," Detective Harrison grumbled to his partner.

"Let's look at the few clues we do have, instead of complaining about those we don't," Detective Palmer suggested.

Harrison flipped open his notebook and ran down the similarities between the numerous disappearances.

"Blood on the floors. Absence of anything pointing to a struggle. No bodies. No ransom notes. And not a single person received any threats beforehand that we know of," Harrison read. "And, of course, except for living in the same small town, there's no connection between the cases."

"What do those things mean? Should we expect more people to disappear? The numbers seem to have dwindled. Are these all kidnappings? Maybe some people took this opportunity to skip out on bad situations. I have no clue what's going on," Palmer concluded in exasperation.

"It's been five days since the initial disappearances occurred and two since the latest ones. The government claims no knowledge of anything and refuses to offer assistance," Harrison grumbled.

"Where does the government think these people have gone? Vacation?"

"Sarcasm, too? This case must really be bugging you," Harrison observed with a chuckle.

"Yeah, it is. If the news reports are right, the number of

missing is staggering. Usually they're only too eager to throw Fibbies our way. Guess they're overwhelmed."

"Too many missing," Palmer agreed. "I wish we had something more to go on, a real clue, anything." Harrison shrugged and returned to studying his notebook.

* * * * *

The men and women seated around the oak table were not smiling. The bald head of the National Security Council stood to face the president.

"Sir, we have a real situation here. The reported missing worldwide now exceeds three hundred million. No country or group claims responsibility. And, frankly, I don't think any one group or country, or even an entire collection of them, could pull off something of this magnitude." The man took his seat.

"Whispers are growing that it's aliens. Any credence to that? What does NASA say?" the president asked.

"NASA, the Russian Federal Space Agency, the private companies, they're all saying the same thing. They see nothing unexplained in the skies."

"So, we have no explanations and no idea if or when our people will return," the president stated the obvious.

"Yes, that is correct, sir," the head of the Department of Homeland Security concurred.

"Ideas?"

Total silence greeted the president's question.

* * * * *

Andrew Mandley was walking down the hallway to his daughter's room when he heard strange voices. He rushed to her room and threw open the door.

"Hello, Mr. Mandley. What's the matter? You look upset," noted Michelle's new nanny.

"I'm fine, but I thought I heard voices," he replied, feeling a little foolish.

"There's nobody here but us," the nanny informed him. Andrew neglected to notice how wide the nanny's eyes were and how mechanical her responses sounded.

"Okay, great." Andrew walked over to his daughter, who was playing with a toy. "Michelle, what have you got there? I've never seen it before. Where did you get it?"

Michelle looked up, distracted from her toy. "It's a spinning top. One of my friends gave it to me," she answered, dismissing her father.

"Which friend?" he inquired.

Michelle stared at him, lips pressed together.

Andrew had never seen her make such a face.

"Daddy, I don't remember. Maybe it was Alexis," she answered, irritated at her father's questions.

Andrew dropped the subject, but regarded his daughter in wonder. She had been acting rather odd for the last week. *I kept telling myself it was sadness and anxiety over her mother's disappearance*, he thought. *Only now I'm not so sure.* He exited her room lost in thought.

"Was your father just in here?" the nanny asked her charge.

"Yes, we were talking about my toys. Why?" Michelle responded.

"I feel like I just woke up. This conversation feels like a dream you can't quite remember. Were you talking to someone else before your father? I thought I heard something."

"Like what?"

The nanny shrugged, rubbing the sleepiness out of her eyes. "I don't know. I guess it was nothing."

Michelle ignored her nanny's musings and returned to her own thoughts.

* * * * *

"What are you saying, Mr. Mandley?" Detective Harrison asked. "That your daughter is involved with these disappearances."

"No, of course not," Andrew protested. "I'm not saying that at all. She's only a six-year-old child."

"Then what are you trying to say?" Detective Palmer asked.

"I'm suggesting she may have seen something that night." Andrew shrugged. "I know it sounds strange, but she's been acting different."

"Look," Harrison said, not unkindly. "I know you're upset at your wife's disappearance, but don't lay your frustration on your daughter." He raised his hand to silence

Heather Silvio

Andrew's renewed protests. "She's still dealing with the fact that her mother is missing. Not to mention half of her neighborhood. It's only natural she's acting unusual. If she wasn't, then I'd be worried," Harrison concluded.

"Naturally she'd be upset," Andrew tried again. "But I'm telling you, she knows something. I know she saw or heard something that night." He crossed his arms over his chest.

"Fine," Palmer agreed reluctantly. "We'll question her again soon. Is that alright with you?" Andrew nodded grimly. Palmer sighed. "Goodbye, Mr. Mandley. Please call my direct line at the station the next time you wish to discuss the case. Don't call dispatch."

Andrew glared at the detectives' backs as they left his home. *Why couldn't they talk to Michelle now?* He knew they preferred not to make house calls, but that was why he had asked them here. He wanted them to talk to Michelle now. He wished he could go out and help search for his wife and the others. Frustration from his inability to do so rolled off of him in nearly palpable waves.

* * * * *

"We got another call about a strange van roaming the area," Detective Palmer reported. "I think we should investigate. Maybe it's connected to our case. What do you think?" he asked Harrison.

"What... oh, yes. How about during lunch?" Detective Harrison looked distracted.

"You okay, pal? You seem confused," Palmer observed.

Harrison stared blankly at him, then responded. He seemed to be listening to something in his head. "I'm fine. Just thinking about the case. Do you ever feel like the answer to your question is right on the tip of your tongue, but you can't quite get it out?" Without waiting for an answer, Harrison stood and walked to the door of the station. "Let's investigate now."

Without another word, they left.

"There it is." Palmer pointed to a white van in the intersection. "That's the van everyone's calling about."

"Right. Let's get it." Harrison floored the gas pedal, flipping on the lights and siren. The van increased its speed and raced away, but the squad car kept pace.

After several blocks the van slowed, then stopped. It pulled over. The detectives stepped out of their car and cautiously approached the mysterious van.

"License and registration," Palmer ordered when he reached the driver's open window. He did a double take: for a moment, the people in the van had appeared to waver. Palmer shook his head and stared at the occupants.

"What seems to be the problem, Officer?" the driver inquired. Although he smiled at them, it seemed out of place on his face.

Not smiling, Harrison answered with a question. "Why did you take off when we approached?"

"How were we to know you were after us? You were in an unmarked car," the passenger of the van responded.

"We had a flashing light and sirens; plus, the road was virtually empty. Who did you think we were after?" Palmer asked her dryly.

"You're right," the driver agreed. "Sorry to trouble you. Here are my license and registration," he said, handing over the documents. Palmer handed them around the front of the van to Harrison to run through the computer.

"Open the van. I want to see what you're hauling." Palmer glared at them, his tone hostile.

The driver's expression hardened. "Do you have a search warrant?"

"I have probable cause," Palmer responded.

"Of what?"

The passenger startled at the driver's question. "Don't be so argumentative," she said to the driver. "It's not a big deal." She redirected her gaze to Palmer. "I'm happy to open the van," she said, fixing her eyes on him. He shuddered.

"Here you go," the passenger said cheerfully, swinging the back doors open. Peering in the open van, Palmer saw an array of expensive technical equipment.

Harrison approached, face set. "Where did you get your paperwork?" he demanded, directing the question to the driver of the van, who had followed his passenger to the rear. "I want an explanation for why you aren't in the computer. If the answer isn't good, I'll take you in and impound your vehicle," Harrison said, as he always believed in the criminal's right to know what was about to happen.

Identical looks of surprise flickered on the couple's faces. "What do you mean, we're not in the computer?" the driver asked, agitated by the news.

"Detective Harrison. Answer please," a tinny voice from nowhere requested. Harrison headed toward their car.

"What is all this for?" asked Palmer. "I've seen some of this before, but most of that equipment looks like it's from another planet." The couple exchanged amused glances, which Palmer missed.

"Most of it is for communications work, and the rest is experimental," the man explained. "For proprietary reasons, I can't tell you exactly what they're for," he added, sensing Palmer's unasked question.

Harrison walked back over to the trio. "I wish to extend my sincere apologies for my harsh behavior. We've located your files. You can go." He handed back the papers.

"Thank you very much," the man replied. "We appreciate your apology. If you will excuse us, we're in a bit of a hurry. We're doing explorations with sound for our boss. See you around." Waving goodbye, he and the woman got into the van.

Palmer and Harrison returned to their car. "What happened with the papers?" Palmer asked.

"I don't know. One minute the people don't exist, the next they have perfect records and I'm being ordered to let them go."

"You should have seen the crap in the back of that van. I looked at some of that stuff and I had no idea what it was." Palmer described several pieces with as much detail as he could remember. "I'm pretty familiar with electronics, but I was clueless about that stuff."

"We had to let them go anyway," Harrison acknowledged. "They had a legitimate reason for wandering around the neighborhood. I'm curious what their experiments are," he wondered aloud.

"I have no idea. Let's go back to the office," Palmer suggested, starting the car.

* * * * *

"Honey, it's time—" Andrew stopped as he surveyed the room. The nanny was asleep on the bed and Michelle was talking into her spinning top. Oblivious to her surroundings, she spoke in a language unrecognizable to him. In fact, he wondered if such a language even existed. Michelle concluded her business and walked over to her desk, placing the top inside. She turned around and saw her father.

"Yes, Daddy?" she asked, masking her surprise.

"What were you doing? Who were you talking to?"

Michelle laughed self-consciously. "I was talking to myself. You know how I do that sometimes," she explained. Andrew just looked at her. She had never talked to herself in her life, even as a babbling baby.

"Okay, sweetie," he agreed, ruffling her hair. She pulled away slightly. Andrew frowned. Michelle turned away from him and began playing with a doll. He stared at her a moment longer before leaving.

* * * * *

"Andrew, it's good to see you," Dr. Pine said, grasping Andrew's hand after entering the Mandley home. He looked at Michelle. "How are you, honey?" She stared at him in stony silence. She and the doctor took their seats on the couch while Andrew remained standing a few feet away. He nervously watched the doctor speak to his daughter. He hoped the hypnotism succeeded, despite his daughter's youth.

"Michelle, you know Dr. Pine. Say hello," Andrew urged her. She stared at her father, then looked warily at the doctor.

"Hello," she whispered. Andrew relaxed.

"Let's get started," the doctor suggested. Andrew nodded. "Michelle, how do you feel?" Dr. Pine asked after hypnotizing her. She looked dreamily at him.

"Everything is fine," she said in an unfamiliar voice. "The charade is over. I—" She clutched her throat before collapsing, unconscious.

"Michelle!" Andrew cried out, rushing to his daughter's side. "Michelle!"

* * * * *

"Red alert, this is a red alert," the dispassionate voice intoned.

"What's the problem?" the captain questioned a guard.

"Someone is cross-linking the bio-room with the transporter," the guard responded.

"Security!" the captain yelled. "Get in there and stop that transport!" The security team ran down the long, metallic-gray hallway to the transporter unit. They reached the unit as the traitor depressed the final button. Guilty but peaceful eyes met with the head of security seconds before a stream of liquid contacted her chest. The guards stared at their wounded prisoner.

* * * * *

"—the safe behind the picture," an old woman cried out, cowering under the sheets. Then she saw that she was alone. "I must be going crazy," she mumbled, falling back asleep.

All over town, and all over the world, the people were returned to their homes, businesses, and churches. Every person kidnapped was returned with no memory of the experience and each spy had been yanked back to the ship orbiting Earth, undetected.

* * * * *

"Michelle, wake up," Andrew begged, tears streaming down his face. He would not lose his daughter after losing his wife. Michelle's eyes fluttered open.

"Daddy," she said weakly. "What's the matter? Why are you crying?"

Andrew cried in relief, hugging his daughter. Michelle looked disoriented and would have no memory of being inhabited and used (neither would any of the others). She would remember none of the incidents of the past week.

A woman appeared in her nightshirt. Her wobbly legs carried her to where her husband and daughter sat on the floor.

"Pamela!" Father and daughter rushed to her side.

"Fresh air," she muttered, barely coherent. Without even considering his actions, Andrew carried his wife through the front door into a world he had not seen in years. As his wife breathed the requested fresh air, Andrew realized he was unafraid. The crushing fear was gone.

* * * * *

"I would like to know what's going on," Detective Harrison complained.

"Yeah, I know what you mean. This has to be the most unusual set of cases I've ever worked or even heard about," Detective Palmer declared.

"What cases? No missing people, no crimes, no cases. That bit of quibbling aside, though, you're right. What a weird bunch of cases," Harrison agreed. "Every single person returned, and no one remembers a thing. It's the strangest thing. I guess it's over and we'll move on to regular disappearances and homicides and stuff." Both men laughed and turned back to case files not related to the numerous disappearances.

* * * * *

The wounded alien sat in the ship's sickbay behind an electromagnetic door. She knew she had no chance of living. Even if she survived the wound inflicted on her by the guard. Not only had she returned the specimens, but she destroyed equipment and years of research. When several guards approached with grim expressions on their faces, that confirmed her belief. Her expression remained impassive and she spoke not a word before they ended her life.

A lone ship exited the atmosphere of a world unaware of its near destruction, the way it entered, to begin planning the experiment again.

The Knight

"Great spirit, creator,
Father of my people.
Spirits of the dead,
Return the wanderer."

An old native concluded the ritual chant and waited for the bear to open her eyes. Only minutes before, the bear laid still. He remembered with distaste the scene he had come upon...

Blood oozed from the carcass, warm and foul. Smiling with satisfaction, the tall, bearded stranger to the forest surveyed his work. *Victory, at last*, he thought to himself. The chase had been exhausting, but he had claimed first prize. What a magnificent showpiece for his growing collection! The black bear lying still on the ground growled. Startled, the man raised his ax, preparing to finish the job he had thought completed. He would not be denied his due. A twig cracking caught his attention.

The native, who could walk as silently as if on feathers, had purposely alerted the murderous intruder. He wanted the man to be aware of his impending destruction. Passive acceptance of those who would strip the Earth of her creatures would no longer be tolerated.

The stranger whirled around in time to glimpse the avenger before being eradicated. An arrow shot forward, straight to its target. As the arrow pierced his eye, the stranger felt an exquisite pain erupt within him. But it was a brief pain, for the arrow that took his eye also claimed his life. The native approached the lifeless bear. Kneeling, he placed his hand over the bear's eyes and chanted…

As the native recalled that earlier scene, the bear's eyes fluttered open. She acknowledged her savior with an inquisitive tilt of her head before gracefully loping off into the forest as if nothing of importance had happened. The native, the knight of the forest, turned slowly and walked off in the direction he had appeared, never looking back.

Taking

Kneeling in the freshly turned earth,
Scent of early dew all around.
The stillness of the morning air
Accents the coffin in the ground.

differences have no meaning
    now,
as tears form and slide
    down my face.
my cheeks are damp with the
    sorrow
of a life gone
    without a trace.

Simple wood – four walls of a box,
Holding within them the living?
But the box holds only death
Always taking, never giving.

Ever After

Marissa Willow came to the beach house to die. She vividly remembered the moment when she decided. After fighting for so long, she would fight no longer.

The one-story cottage caught Marissa's eye the instant the realtor set the picture on the table in front of her and her parents. A weathered, but immaculately maintained, off-white house with all the amenities she required. She expected the six-month lease would outlast her. At 17 years old, that was scary to contemplate, but she would always be grateful to her mom and dad for fulfilling her last wish. They'd said the money earmarked for college studies she would never begin was hers to spend.

Marissa walked through the front door and placed her two oversized roller bags beside her. The front room, a combination living/dining room, contained minimal furnishings. Sunlight streaming through the bay windows bathed a small couch and end table. She took a deep breath of the ocean air, grabbed the handles for her bags, and walked across the room to her new bedroom. One chest of drawers and a four-poster bed filled the space. Heaving both suitcases onto the bed, Marissa crossed to the window and pulled open the blinds. She closed her eyes and allowed the rays of light to warm her chilled skin.

Deciding to leave the unpacking until the sun set, Marissa walked through the back door to the outside and onto the beach. Mere inches from the water's edge, she sprawled out in the sand, staring up into the cloudless azure sky. *This is beautiful*, she thought wistfully, before dozing off. In her dreams, she relived her torturous years of existence.

Honestly, the first five were wonderful. Marissa lived and played like any other little girl. Then came the bruises that would not heal and the exhaustion that nearly incapacitated the normally vivacious child. The C-word had invaded her life, not just her body. Repeated trips to the hospital for chemotherapy, nausea so bad she would have preferred death, and, finally, remission. For a brief while, life would return to a close approximation of normal. Until the cycle began again, over and over, ultimately bringing her to the beach.

As the sun set, Marissa woke up. She walked back

towards the house, brushing sand off in the thirty seconds it took to reach the door. Feeling dehydrated, she went into the kitchen.

"Who's there?" Marissa stood in the center of the kitchen, pivoting around to see the person she had glimpsed upon entering. No one was in the room with her, but she would have sworn she had seen a tall, blond man standing by the refrigerator, next to the window.

"Just the sun fooling with my eyes," she decided, and dismissed the image. After pouring a glass of water, Marissa walked out through the back door to the porch. She settled into the rocking chair to watch the sun finish falling beyond the horizon.

Marissa opened her eyes and saw it was still light out. The quality of the light and the pain in her body relayed the message to her that it was not *still* light out, but a new day dawning. She had fallen asleep on the porch and missed her scheduled dose of pain medication. The doctor had admitted nothing could be done to cure her, but she could avoid an agonizingly painful death. Thus far, medication controlled the pain. *If I remember to take my meds*, she ruefully reminded herself. She stretched her aching body and returned to the house, heading straight for the bathroom.

After emerging from a refreshing shower, Marissa prepared breakfast. She noted that she was already losing her appetite, but she ate the entire meal.

"Hi, Mom. It's me. I'm just calling to see how you and Dad are doing. And, to let you know I'm moved in to the beach house. Give me a call when—" Marissa stopped as someone on the other end picked up.

"Marissa, are you there?" Audrey Willow asked.

"Yes, Mom. I'm here." Marissa could hear fumbling noises on the other end of the line.

"How are you feeling? Are you in a lot of pain? I don't understand why you wanted to live away from your family at a time like this..."

Marissa tuned out as her mother rattled on for a few minutes. She knew the spiel backwards and forwards. She could never explain to her mother why she needed to be alone right now. Later, when the end neared, she would want her family around.

Silence on the line reminded Marissa that conversation required two people to work. "Sorry, Mom. I spaced for a second. What did you say?" Marissa heard her mother's heavy sigh.

"You haven't been listening to a word I've said."

"Yes, I have," Marissa protested weakly.

"Why do you even bother to call if you aren't going to listen to anything I say?"

Marissa's eyes teared up. She wiped at them with the back of her hand before responding. "I wanted to talk to you, that's all."

Audrey heard the catch in her daughter's voice. "What's

wrong? Something's wrong. Dad and I can be out there on the next flight."

"No, Mom. I'm fine. You and Dad don't need to come out, yet." Her parents knew she would call for them, and her sister, Debra, when the time neared. "Everything is fine. It's just a little overwhelming to think about. I've moved to paradise to die." Marissa allowed herself a dry chuckle at that thought. When Audrey didn't respond, Marissa knew the call had to end. "I'm sorry, Mom. I didn't call to upset you."

"I know that, dear. Your father wants to talk to you." Audrey handed the phone to her husband.

"How are you feeling, sweetheart? Are you sure everything is okay?" Steve gripped the phone, as if by having the device closer, he could be closer to his daughter.

Marissa spent the next ten minutes explaining to her father all the things she had discussed with her mother. She hung up the phone both uplifted and drained.

Her parents had feared this time would come since her first diagnosis as a child. They were handling it the best they could. Better than Debra was handling the situation. Marissa didn't even bother calling Debbie to see how she was doing. Ever since Marissa received her *death sentence*, Debbie had been extremely uncomfortable interacting with her. It saddened Marissa, and she hoped Debbie would overcome her apprehensions and fly out at the end with their parents.

Marissa left the kitchen and headed toward the door. She wanted to spend as much time in the sun as she had left. Marissa stopped in her tracks and stared at the young man standing by the living room window. He took no notice of her as he stared out. She studied his profile instead of going for help. He didn't appear to be a threat. The man was tall, well over her own 5'5". About her age, he had similar blond hair like hers, but with curls throughout, while her hair wouldn't recognize a curl.

The man turned to face Marissa. His dark green eyes probed her blue ones, even from across the room. She took a step forward and he was gone. He didn't leave, but simply vanished. Marissa blinked several times, staring at the spot he had occupied, and willed him to return. When he refused to reappear, she felt oddly forlorn. Obviously, the man wasn't real, or he wouldn't have vanished. And, yet... Marissa remembered the fleeting glimpse from before of a man in the kitchen. It had to be the same guy, but she still had no explanation for him appearing at all. Was he real, a ghost, or a figment of her imagination?

Marissa crossed the room to where he had stood. She would have sworn it felt warmer, more lived in, right there. Of course, the sun came through the window the strongest in that spot. She was perplexed and intrigued. "I'll just do my normal routine until you return," she announced to the room in a voice more confident than she felt. Here, at last, was something to take her mind off of dying.

Continuing her interrupted walk to the outside, Marissa tried to rid herself of thoughts of the blond man. For the rest of that day, in fact, he would not leave her alone. She read a book by the ocean, ate dinner, and thought about a certain blond man who may or may not exist. She knew without a doubt he would haunt her dreams that night.

The next day dawned sunny and bright. And the day after that. And still several more, all without a sign of the blond man. Marissa was no longer certain she had seen anything at all. Until the morning he returned.

Marissa had eaten breakfast, although not nearly enough, she admitted to herself, and was walking on the warm sand when she saw him by the water. She hastened her steps, no longer enthralled by the feel of sand between her toes. She stopped ten feet away and waited for him to disappear again. Instead, he spoke.

"Hello, Marissa." The modulated voice had a lilting musical quality.

"You know my name," she responded in awe.

"Don't you remember me?"

"Remember you? I've never met you. I've come to the conclusion that you're a figment of my drugged imagination." He surprised her by laughing. "What are you laughing at?" The question was one of bewilderment, not hurt.

"What makes you think I'm not real?"

"Real people don't vanish at will," she pointed out.

"True, but that doesn't answer my question."

"Now you've lost me," Marissa admitted.

"I can still be real, without being a real person," he explained.

She chuckled. "Okay, that made perfect sense. Would you care to explain so that this *real person* can understand?"

"I exist differently from your conception of a real person, but that doesn't make me less real."

"If you're real, but not a real person, what are you?" Now Marissa was fully drawn into the man standing before her. On some level, she believed him, but she also felt like Alice falling down the rabbit hole. Regardless, he captivated her. "Who are you?"

"I can't explain the situation so you'll understand. The closest thing is that I'm a spirit. I exist outside of a physical body."

"Where do you exist? How do you feel? How did you get here?" Marissa halted her rapid-fire questioning at his raised hand.

"I exist in another dimension, but while I'm here, I feel everything you do. The wind, ocean, and sun."

"You didn't say how you got here."

"You brought me here."

"I did?" Marissa asked in disbelief. "I don't even know your name. How could I bring you here?"

"All the same, you did. My name is Chris." He watched her reaction as he revealed his name.

A memory stirred in Marissa at the revelation of his name and she was well aware of the intensity of his stare.

Chris could see that his name alone was not enough. "You still don't remember me?"

"I... don't know. Something is there, but I can't access it," Marissa confessed. "Why don't you tell me?"

"I'll let your subconscious tackle the question of my identity. I didn't look like this when we knew each other, but you should still sense who I am," Chris said.

"Can't you tell me anything concrete? When would I have met you? How long did we know each other?" Marissa cursed her inability to remember anything farther than a few years in the past without constant reminders of the event.

"Those are all questions for another day, Marissa." And with a quick smile, he vanished.

"You really need to stop doing that," she grumbled.

Time passed, with Marissa not remembering, and Chris not reappearing. Sometimes, upon awakening, or in that time between waking and sleeping, an idea would surface. Trying to grab the idea and hold on only pushed it away. Her weakening condition forced her to take higher dosages of pain medication. She began to give up hope and believed she would die before she found the answer that would bring Chris back. She realized her feelings for him were stronger than for anyone she had ever known. He had awakened a deep reserve of feeling she didn't even know existed, including the belief that she had indeed known him since time began.

Children's laughter filled the air and a little girl ran toward the monkey bars. Marissa stared at the little girl for a full minute before she realized she was staring at herself. She vaguely remembered the preschool playground her younger self currently occupied, but not any specific incidences. The young girl dropped off the bars and turned in Marissa's direction. A big smile appeared and Marissa wondered if the little girl could see her.

"Chris!" *Marissa started as the little girl hollered the unexpected name. In astonishment, Marissa watched as a little blond boy ran from behind her and toward the girl. Chris grabbed the little girl excitedly by the arm and pulled her off toward the seesaw. As Marissa watched the children playing, a flood of memories surfaced.*

Chris Freeman had been her best friend and constant companion from the moment they were born in adjoining hospital rooms, until... what? Marissa could not remember what had separated them, only that she had no memories of Chris beyond preschool. At age 5, he had vanished from her life.

Marissa woke up crying from a sense of loss she didn't understand. She remembered the dream, unusual for her, but could conclude nothing from it. Perhaps Chris had moved away with his family before kindergarten. She made a mental note to ask him, the next time he appeared.

If there was a next time.

"Hello?" Marissa knew her voice sounded frail and hated the pity she was sure would be on the other end of the line.

"Is that you, Marissa?"

"Debbie?"

"It's me, your big sister," Debbie sang out, in forced good cheer. "I was calling to see how you're doing. I hadn't heard from you since you made the big move." Her voice dropped to a whisper. "You don't sound so good."

"Well, I'm not dead, yet! I still have a month or so." *Or maybe less*, she thought, and a dry laugh escaped her.

"That's not funny." Debbie's voice sounded thick, as if she were about to cry. "Have you seen a doctor lately? How do you know it's only a month?"

"I haven't timed it to the day, you know. That's just how it feels. And, no, I haven't gone to a doctor."

Debbie's end of the phone fell silent. After a minute, Marissa started to say goodbye.

"Wait, Marissa, I...," Debbie faltered. "I'd like to come out there next week, if you don't mind."

Marissa's mind flashed on to Chris, wondering if he would appear with her sister present in the house, before responding to Debbie's request. "Of course, you can come out here. I won't be doing any entertaining, but you're always welcome. You know that." Marissa could hear Debbie weeping and she felt her own throat tighten.

Coughing, Marissa cleared her throat and asked if Debbie had the address for the beach house.

"Yes, I have your address. I'll see you next week. I love you, little sister." Debbie's voice broke and she hurriedly hung up the phone.

"I love you, too," Marissa responded into the silence.

"Don't cry, Marissa."

Marissa turned at the sound of his voice, elated he had returned. "I'm so glad you came back. I remembered who you are!" Marissa told him triumphantly. Chris frowned, but it disappeared so fast Marissa wasn't sure if it had been there at all.

"Tell me what you remember about me."

Marissa told him about the playground in her dream and the triggered memories.

"You don't remember why we stopped playing together," Chris stated.

"Well, no, but I assumed you moved away." Seeing his expression, she hurried on, "Is it that important?"

"Yes, it is. Try to remember, Marissa," Chris urged.

"I did try," Marissa snapped back, frustrated by her inability to remember. "Sorry. I'm not mad at you. I'm mad at my Swiss cheese memory."

"Let's try another tactic. A visualization technique might work."

Marissa nodded her assent, so Chris continued.

"Sit down in the chair. Is that chair comfortable

enough? Okay, good. Close your eyes. Think back to the last time you remember seeing me."

"That day on the playground when we were five."

"Play out that day and see where it takes you."

Marissa described that day for almost half an hour before her voice faltered. "Your mother, uh, arrived to take us both home. We didn't want to leave, but she was in a hurry. She picked up some artwork we had done earlier in the afternoon. While we were walking toward the car, a small four-door, she told us how much she liked our drawings. She buckled us in the back seat. You and I kept up a steady stream of inconsequential chatter, as she, uh, backed the car up and left the parking lot. I... I'm not sure what happened next. It's kind of fuzzy." Marissa stopped and gave a little shrug.

"You're doing great. Keep trying. You're almost there." Chris reached over the table and took her hand in his. "Keep trying," he repeated.

Closing her eyes again, Marissa tried to remember what happened. "All I see is a road, we're just driving along. Wait, we're coming upon an intersection. I can see between the front seats that the red light turns green right before we enter the intersection. And, then... oh, my god. A van is headed straight for us! It's too late for anybody to get out of the way. The accident is moving in slow motion. I can see the driver of the van, his mouth and eyes opening in surprise as he crashes into the side of the car. I feel pain, a horrible wrenching pain, and then, nothing." Tears rolled down Marissa's face. She kept her eyes closed tight.

"Then what happened?"

"I just told you I blacked out. Nothing else. Wait, that's not true. I remember standing next to you in a lush meadow that seemed too beautiful to be real. You took my hand and led me toward an opening into a wooded area. *It's time*, you said. A bright flash of light obscured everything for a moment. When it faded, you and the meadow were transparent. You were frowning. The bright flash of light occurred again, followed by darkness." Marissa paused, eyes closed and brow furrowed in concentration, trying to remember.

"I woke up in a hospital bed. You and your mother were dead, and I had spent the last forty-eight hours in a coma. You... were... dead," she repeated, disliking the taste of the words in her mouth. She tightened her grip on his hand and opened her teary eyes to see a look of sorrow in his own. "You didn't move. You died."

"Yes."

"And so did I."

"Yes. The bright light you described was from the shocks the doctor used to restart your heart."

"I wasn't supposed to live, was I?"

"No, you weren't. I'm sorry."

"My first diagnosis of cancer came right after I started kindergarten. I've suffered my entire life, because they wouldn't let me die," Marissa spoke in a calm voice, though her eyes glittered with anger.

"They didn't know," Chris tried to soothe her. When her expression didn't change, Chris changed his approach. "You got to live. Maybe your life hasn't been perfect, but you're surrounded by people who love you and—"

"Do you see anybody else present?" Marissa cut him off. She knew her anger was misplaced; being here alone now had been her choice.

"You know what I mean. Life is a gift. You were given the opportunity to hang on to it for a little while longer than you should have. That was a blessing, not a curse."

"A blessing. I've spent my blessed life in a hospital, nauseated and in pain!"

Chris took Marissa's face in his hands. "Whether you want to admit it or not, the fact remains that your life was a blessing. I didn't get that chance. Get past the anger and suffering and think of your family and friends. Think of all the things you were able to experience when you weren't in the hospital. Your body accelerated your dying as soon as you awoke from the accident, yes, but you held on for twelve years. You must have liked something in your life to hold on to it this long."

"You're right, of course." Marissa offered a wavering smile. She stood unsteadily and went to the window. "The fight is over, isn't it?" She turned to face Chris. "That's why you're here."

"Yes."

"How much time do I have?"

"About two weeks."

"I guess I better say my goodbyes."

Chris nodded, then stood and disappeared again. Marissa remained silent for a minute. "You are quite the hallucination," she announced to the empty room, although she knew he was as real as anyone else.

Marissa was sitting on the front patio when Debra arrived in a cab from the airport. Fatigue kept Marissa from standing to greet her sister, but she managed a smile from where she sat. Her smile showed surprise when she saw two more passengers alight from the taxi.

"Hi, sweetheart. We hope you don't mind us dropping in a week early like this, but when Deb said she was coming out now, we decided to tag along." Audrey Willow looked uncomfortable. Marissa knew her mother was waiting to be chastised for her 'rude' behavior.

"I'm glad you came," Marissa said, instead of berating her parents. In truth, she *was* glad to see them. "Hi, Dad."

Steve Willow leaned over to give his daughter a hug. "You're skin and bones, girl. Have you been eating?"

"Sorry, Dad. I haven't had much of an appetite lately. It's good you came now."

"Deb told us you didn't sound well on the phone. We were worried we might not get to say goodbye," Audrey explained, crying.

Marissa stood, fighting the wave of nausea that gripped her. She walked into the house, gesturing that her family should follow. She sat at the kitchen table. "Mom and Dad, you get the spare room. Deb, you'll have to sleep on the couch. I don't know if extra sets of towels came with the house; check the hall closet. I only brought one extra set."

"That's okay, honey. You know me, I brought along all my own supplies. I have enough for Deb, too," Audrey added.

"Thanks, Mom." Debbie glanced at her sister, whose head was drooping toward the table with every passing second. "Looks like somebody could use a nap."

"I think I'll lie on the beach. Make yourselves at home. If it gets dark and I haven't come back in, somebody please wake me up," Marissa requested.

"No problem. Let me help you." Audrey placed an arm around Marissa to help her to her feet. After walking out the back door, Marissa kissed her mother's cheek. Audrey watched Marissa take wobbling steps to the water's edge, then stretch out on a blanket in the sand. Audrey cried heavier. Steve and Debbie walked up beside her and put their arms around her. She offered no resistance when they led her back into the house.

"I see your family has arrived," Chris noted, with a nod towards the house. Marissa beamed as he approached her and took a seat next to her in the sand.

"Yeah, they're here. I invited Deb, and my parents showed up, too. I think they fear the end is near," Marissa added.

"It is near."

"Don't you think I know that. I'm the one dying. You don't have to remind me of it every time you see me," Marissa snapped.

"My being here is reminder enough, isn't it?"

"You're the Angel of Death, are you not?"

"No, I'm not. You know I'm not. Why are you angry with me?" Chris looked perplexed.

"I don't want to die," Marissa whispered, avoiding his eyes.

"There's no need to be embarrassed. Not wanting to die is normal. Most people dislike and fear what they don't understand."

"That's just it. I *could* understand if you would tell me."

"It doesn't work that way. The survival of life depends on the mystery of death," Chris explained.

"Don't feed me a line of bull. I am a dying woman, not a philosopher. You came to me, remember? The least you could do is give me a clue," Marissa begged.

Chris remained silent for a moment. "All I can tell you is that existence in the afterlife is not at all like life here. Dying isn't the end of life, it's a transfer of energy to another mode of being."

"That cleared it right up," Marissa muttered.

Chris looked pained. "Think of death as your life force moving into another realm," he tried again to explain.

"Never mind," she sighed. "I was never into science fiction. If you say death is not the end and is nothing to fear, then I believe you. I love you." Marissa appeared startled by her own admission. Chris mouthed the words back at her. Hearing a noise, she looked over her shoulder at the beach house, in time to see her sister walk back inside. Marissa looked back at Chris. "I think I may have a problem." Chris nodded in agreement.

Marissa entered the house to find three solemn faces staring at her. She felt like a freak in a circus side show and preempted their *you're insane* lectures. "What do you think you heard out there, Deb?"

Debra exchanged glances with their parents before answering. "It sounded like you were talking to someone who wasn't present."

Audrey jumped in to offer Marissa a chance to explain. "I told them you had a perfectly reasonable explanation. That you weren't talking to yourself at all. Here, honey, have a seat." She gave Marissa her chair.

"Thanks, Mom. No, I wasn't talking to myself or someone who wasn't there," Marissa assured her family.

"We're so relieved to hear you say that," Steve interjected.

Marissa ignored the interruption. "I was talking to Chris."

"Who? There was no one out there with you," Debbie objected.

"Not that you could see," Marissa stated, bracing for the reaction.

Silence filled the room, then a chorus of voices denied, cajoled, and otherwise tried to get Marissa to take back her statement. Audrey chose to humor her deluded daughter.

"Who is Chris and where did you meet him?" Audrey asked in a pleasant voice, such as people use in mental hospitals.

"Actually, all of you know him, too. We went to school together as children," Marissa hurried on before anyone could interrupt. "His name is Christopher Freeman."

Steve and Debbie didn't recognize the name, but Marissa could tell her mother did. "Chris Freeman died when you were a child. I'm surprised you remember him at all," Audrey said.

"I didn't. Until he appeared in a dream. I began seeing him while I was awake, and, soon, we started talking."

"I don't know what to say to that," Audrey admitted.

"None of you have to say anything. I'm going into the living room. Judging by the smell, dinner is almost ready. For the first time in a long time, I'm hungry. Please yell for me when it's done. Remember, the walls aren't that thick. When you talk about my delusions, whisper," Marissa admonished them with a wink before leaving the room.

"It's a hallucination, maybe caused by the drugs,"

Debbie speculated. "Have you seen the amount of pain medication she's taking?"

"Do you think we should call her doctor, or a local doctor? Talking to a person who has been dead nearly thirteen years can't be good for her," Audrey said.

"Why isn't it good for her?" Audrey and Debbie stared at Steve like he'd grown a second head. "Listen to me before you start yapping. You've seen Marissa. She's got days, maybe a week, left. I'm sure she's frightened. If having this fantasy relationship with her dead friend reassures her and comforts her, then who are we to interfere? Whether her vision is real or not is irrelevant. For all we know, he is real. I don't have the answer to what happens when we die, and neither do the two of you. I say we go along with her belief," Steve concluded.

"You may have a point about her conversations providing comfort and reassurance," Audrey concurred. "I agree to go along with her."

"Chris is as real as you or me, even if he's a figment of Marissa's imagination," Debbie added in summation.

"Are you planning to sleep through another day?" Debbie called out playfully before peeking into Marissa's bedroom. Marissa had not gotten out of bed, except to go to the bathroom, in the past twenty-four hours. When Debbie didn't get a reply, she walked over to the bed. Her sister was so still, Debbie worried Marissa was no longer alive. Then she saw Marissa's chest rise and fall. Debbie exhaled sharply in relief, unaware she'd been holding her breath. Marissa's eyes opened.

"Go get Mom and Dad," Marissa whispered, her voice nearly inaudible. Debbie left the room and returned with their parents.

"Are you okay, sweetie?" Audrey asked, not wanting to hear the answer she already knew in her heart.

"It's almost over now," Marissa responded. Her eyes moved around the room, searching.

"Do you need something? I'll go get it," Steve volunteered, in a desperate attempt to feel useful. Marissa appeared to not have heard. Her lips moved, but no sound emerged. Audrey leaned in closer, hoping to understand what her daughter was trying to say.

"Where's... Chris?... Chris?... Chris?" Marissa repeated over and over again. Audrey clasped her hands to her mouth to stifle the sound of her sudden sobbing. Suddenly, Marissa stopped trying to talk and smiled. "Everybody's... here... now," she said, though with great effort.

"We're here for you, honey," Audrey assured her dying daughter. Steve and Debbie echoed the sentiment.

"You didn't think I would abandon you now, did you?" Chris asked with a sad smile.

"I knew you'd come," she replied. "Mom and Dad... you were the best... parents I could ever... have wished for," Marissa began slowly. "Deb, you were... always... my favorite sister."

"I'm your only sister," Debbie responded to the familiar line, tears streaming down her face.

"Marissa, it's time now," Chris told her.

"I love you," she whispered with her final breath.

Marissa's family later swore they heard an unknown man's voice respond along with their own voices.

"I love you, too, Marissa."

God?

Hymns and prayers
Sinners repent

Who is your savior?
Chant and confess

Blind masses led
Lambs of innocence?

Naiveté and ignorance
God does not exist.

Revenge

The man looked up from his counter at the stunning blond. She spoke before he had the thought to offer to help.

"I'm here to pick up my gun," she informed him in a low, throaty voice.

"I'll need to see some identification," he responded, sounding apologetic to his own ears. The blond removed her driver's license from her purse and placed it on the counter. Victoria Horowitz.

Jack whistled appreciatively as he checked out the gun in storage at the back of the store. The Beretta 93 R, with its selective fire, was a mighty effective mini-submachine gun. The woman had taste, he admitted, even if the gun seemed strong for her. He brought the gun, case, and extra ammunition over to the counter where Victoria stood immobile. Her icy demeanor stopped him from speaking. He accepted her credit card and wordlessly finished the transaction for her purchase. The blond picked up the gun and supplies, put them in her purse, and walked to the door of the store.

"You can't take that out in your purse," Jack protested.

"It's just until I get home," she said with a wink, and Jack remained silent as she left the store. He was just a clerk, after all.

"Hey, Vikki, where have you been? Borr and his minions are in a snit over you," a fellow worker informed her when she walked through the office door.

Victoria grinned and replied, "I can handle him." The other employee shrugged and returned to his work. Victoria entered Borr's office holding her purse in her left hand as naturally as a woman about to shoot her boss could. Upon seeing her, Borr began yelling.

"Do you want to keep working here? If so, maybe you had better explain why you missed work the past two weeks without bothering to call! You used to be such a fantastic worker. I don't know what's happened, but I want an explanation. And how come you're two hours late today? I suppose I should be happy that you bothered to show up at all!" Mr. Borr seethed with anger. He always did have a terrible temper. Victoria's next statement only aggravated matters.

"Go to hell," she replied coolly to his angry tirade. He spluttered a little before regaining his voice.

"Get out of my office and clean out your desk." He turned and faced the window. "You are fired. Leave and don't ever come back. Mr. Yorm, show Ms. Horowitz out, please."

"Don't bother, Mr. Yorm. I'm not leaving."

Borr turned from the window, jaw clenched at her refusal to leave.

Victoria trained her gun on the shocked faces of Yorm and Borr. A third man stood to the side, unconcerned by the gun.

Meanwhile, in the outer office, everyone hushed, wondering why the shouting had ceased. A bloodcurdling scream from Borr's office broke the silence. Workers rushed in to see Borr and Yorm under the desk. Eyes widened and pulses quickened as the office workers took in the scene. The new intern fainted.

The bodies of the victims were gone, only the heads remained. Folks looked around for the bodies to no avail. Eventually, all eyes trained on the bloodless heads. An executive assistant finally called the police.

Victoria sat in a corner sobbing. A large bruise on her cheek grew darker every minute. People stumbled every which way, hollering to each other. The police arrived to take control of the situation.

Uniformed officers calmed the wandering and confused

witnesses. After about five minutes, Detectives Michael Palmer and John Harrison arrived.

Palmer had been a homicide detective for five years, yet he'd never witnessed a more chaotic scene than the one before him now (despite the beat cops present). He called in to request the identification section be sent to the scene. Detective Harrison assisted the uniforms with clearing the room while Palmer walked over to sit beside Victoria.

Harrison sent some witnesses to the station to give formal statements, then questioned those who remained. Palmer glanced up from his huddled conversation with Victoria in time to see the Major Crimes Scene Unit arrive – they rarely arrived this quickly.

The ident technicians arrived. They dusted for prints, took photos of the deceased, and collected the other physical evidence. No one seemed disturbed by the missing bodies. Palmer called the station and requested that Victoria be taken into custody and brought to Denison State Hospital for a complete checkup, both physical and mental. Request approved, he called the hospital and explained the situation.

"She's pretty shaken up," Palmer said, glancing back at Victoria. Harrison followed his glance to where Victoria had stopped crying. She stared through the men as though they did not exist, oblivious to her surroundings.

"I've called the boys at Denison to come retrieve Ms. Victoria Horowitz," Palmer told Harrison.

"Is there anything you'd like me to take care of?" Harrison inquired. Palmer shook his head.

"No. Do you sense something wrong? Besides the fact that the bodies are missing. Something about this case already troubles me. It's almost a sense of déjà vu," Palmer told Harrison.

"What could possibly be familiar about this case? We've never had one with missing bodies before."

"I don't know what's familiar. I'm just very uncomfortable about the whole thing. Something feels wrong. In fact, I feel like I'm being watched." Palmer frowned in thought.

Just then two orderlies from Denison State Hospital arrived to take Victoria. Upon noticing them, she shrieked at the top of her lungs. She knew the men operated under the control of another.

"No, no, no, no, no! Don't let them take me! They'll destroy me! I'm trapped! Help me!" She cried out like a woman possessed.

One attendant grabbed Victoria by the arms while the other prepared a syringe he then pushed into her upper arm. The orderlies held her tightly until the sedative took effect. When her breathing slowed and deepened, the attendants hoisted her onto a gurney and carried her away.

A pair of unseen eyes watched the whole scene as it unfolded, both amused and satisfied. *Now I can proceed*, he thought.

Back in the office, forensics finished and removed the heads. The detectives remained behind to complete preliminary questioning of the twenty or so witnesses still in the office. However, it was already obvious to Palmer that nobody had seen anything of importance.

Having watched the orderlies remove Victoria, something about their manners, or lack of them, disturbed Palmer a great deal. He ignored this concern and returned to the big question. Where were the bodies that once belonged to the severed heads? He motioned Harrison over.

"What do you suppose happened to the bodies?" Palmer asked his partner. Harrison glanced around the room before answering.

"I haven't the faintest idea. I guess Ms. Horowitz had an accomplice since she had a gun, not a knife, and she never left the room to dump the bodies."

"Yes," Palmer exhaled slowly. "There's only one exit and nowhere to hide two adult bodies. Everyone saw the victims and Horowitz go in. No one saw them come out. But even an accomplice can't make multiple bodies disappear."

"Point taken," Harrison responded. "We'd better go see Victoria Horowitz."

"Definitely. You finish up here and I'll head over to the hospital," Palmer told him. "I'll meet you in the morning at the station."

Palmer left, waving goodbye to Harrison over his shoulder. He walked down the stairs (healthier than elevators) and over to his car, unaware of the hidden eyes watching his every move.

Palmer sensed something different as he got into his car. Nothing major, a few subtle differences. A slight scent of cologne. No dust on the console display. Then he saw it. A CD, half in his player, that had not previously been there. He leaned over to inspect it. Using his handkerchief, so as not to smudge any fingerprints, he nudged it all the way into the player.

"Hello, Michael. It's been a long time, hasn't it, old buddy," a man's voice on the CD told him. Exuding sarcasm, the voice continued. "No need to be so careful. Do you honestly believe that I would leave a fingerprint? Of course not, I'm too smart for that." The voice chuckled. Long seconds of silence followed.

Palmer was about to stop the CD when the voice proceeded. "Not yet, Michael. I'm not finished. Do you recognize my voice?" Palmer frowned. "I know you don't. It's been years since we spoke. Well, you'll never solve the case without at least a tiny clue." Silence. Palmer leaned till his ear was almost touching the speaker.

"Now that I have your complete attention," the barely audible voice whispered. "Here is your clue: Electricity can kill or give life – which did it give me? That's all. Good luck."

Detective Michael Palmer stared at the CD player. *What a fruitcake*, was his first thought. Something did seem familiar, and Palmer would have sworn he knew the owner of the disembodied voice. Troubled, he hit play again. Silence. He hit eject. The CD had disappeared. *Just like the bodies*, he thought.

"How do the two events relate?" he asked himself. If only he could remember the man who belonged to the voice. He drove to the hospital.

"What do you mean, she's not here?" Palmer asked in disbelief.

"Exactly what I said, sir. We do not have a Victoria Horowitz, nor do we expect her to arrive. Sorry," the receptionist explained again, not sounding sorry.

"I spoke to someone earlier today and this hospital picked her up. I saw the men with my own eyes."

"You would have spoken to me and I never spoke with you. Did you ask who you were speaking to when you called?"

"There's obviously been some miscommunication."

"Obviously." She dismissed him and returned to her paperwork.

"Ma'am, just one more question." She sighed. "Has anyone been here who should not have been? Could you check to see if any of your staff uniforms are missing or otherwise unaccounted for?" Palmer smiled sweetly at her, a smile she did not return.

"I haven't seen anyone strange or unexpected and there is just about no way to locate all the uniforms. Many people keep their uniforms when they quit." Once again, she turned back to her paperwork. Palmer reached across her desk and helped himself to her telephone. Ignoring her sounds of protest, he called the station. After Harrison agreed to send men to comb the hospital and the office building for the missing suspect/witness, Palmer left.

He drove home, continually glancing in his rearview mirror to see if he was being followed. He was not. The man on the CD was nowhere near his car. Palmer checked the entire house for unwanted visitors when he arrived home. After convincing himself he was alone with his cats, he reread his notes from the day and went to bed. A restless night followed. Headless bodies plagued his dreams. And voices, hideous voices, all telling him what he could not hear. The explanation for the murders.

The next morning dawned gray and dreary, matching Palmer's mood. He felt more than a little annoyed that after a night's rest he still wasn't coming up with any new ideas concerning the case. Upon reaching the station that morning, his bad mood escalated. Without discussing the entire CD, he mentioned to Harrison the comment about electricity.

Harrison laughed and replied, "You know, that sounds like something Peter Nulin would have said. Remember him, Michael? What a nut! He used to condescend to you all the time. He was your first death penalty case, wasn't he? For murdering some family, I believe."

"Yeah, I remember Nulin," Palmer mumbled, his mind racing. *Could there be a connection between these murders and Nulin?* Shaking his head in answer to his own inner question, he said goodbye as Harrison left the office. His case had just become more convoluted instead of clearer.

An idea formed in his mind. It was perfect – except for two minor problems. The bodies remained missing and the State electrocuted his main suspect.

The invisible man's clue came to mind. Palmer focused on the second part of the clue. The voice on the CD (Peter Nulin?) had said, "or it can give life." Palmer decided to follow up on this lead, although it seemed improbable (more like impossible) that Nulin could be even connected, let alone personally responsible for the murders.

It could be a copycat, he realized. He zeroed in on this possibility.

Palmer started checking around. He visited the Graveyard first. This was in the police station's basement where they stored files of past cases. Unoccupied when he arrived, he figured no one would care if he had a look around. He smelled something terrible and made a mental note to call housekeeping when he finished.

Palmer went to the files for closed cases at the back of the room. He noted with concern that the smell became stronger and more familiar the closer he came to the filing cabinets. The files were stored alphabetically in several large cabinets. He opened the cabinet L-Q.

"Holy shit!" He found the source of the stench. A dead man sat in the pullout file. To be more precise, part of a dead man sat in the file. It was only from the neck to the abdomen. The stench from the partial corpse told Palmer it had been there days. Or at least the body died days ago.

He donned a pair of latex gloves he kept in his pocket (a habit he carried over from his days as a responding officer). A sliver of white on the body caught his eye. He leaned over and pulled lightly on the object. It was an envelope with his name on it. Removing the envelope was tantamount to stealing evidence, but he justified that the envelope had his name on it and opened it anyway. Inside, folded up, was a note… along with part of Peter Nulin's file!

"I need to sit down," Palmer mumbled. This was bizarre. The evidence pointed to someone knowledgeable about the case. That included any number of police officers, or Peter Nulin. A copycat would not have had access to the old files. *Nobody is down here with me and I could have been anyone*, he reminded himself. *How could the person involved know that I'd find the body and get the clue?* His musings almost caused him to miss the soft clink as something fell from the body to the floor of the cabinet.

Intrigued, he stood back up and cautiously approached the file cabinet. Peering down past the body to the bottom of the cabinet, Palmer discovered another CD that appeared identical. He reached in and picked it up. After pocketing the letter and the CD, he called upstairs.

"This is Palmer down in Graveyard. I discovered the partial remains of a body. Tell Harrison to get down here with some men." He hung up and walked over to the body.

In record time, Harrison arrived in the basement with two officers. Palmer pointed to the torso. Soon the Graveyard was crawling with people. The head of the ident team approached Palmer. "I assume no one has touched anything or disturbed the body at all?" he inquired.

"No one's been down here since I found it moments ago," he evaded. Harrison, who witnessed the exchange, knew Palmer was hiding something. He proved his hunch correct when Palmer asked to speak with him in his office in ten minutes.

In the office exactly ten minutes later, Palmer motioned for Harrison to take a seat. Harrison suspected he would not like what he was about to hear. Palmer removed the envelope and CD from his pocket. Harrison's face remained neutral as he asked, "What are those?"

"Those," Palmer replied, "I removed from the body." Before Harrison could question further, Palmer hurried to explain. "They pertain to me, which is why I removed them." Looking at the desk, he continued. "Someone sent them, I believe, in connection to a dead man." He opened a partial file. "Peter Nulin."

"What's going on, Mike?"

"Let me explain and you tell me if I'm crazy or imagining things. It all began four years ago on March 3. It was my shift and I was patrolling my area," he started the story. "Anyway, I entered a suburb at just past noon. Suddenly, I heard rapid gunfire. I arrived at a two-story house at about the same time a masked man with an automatic was leaving."

"Peter Nulin," Harrison guessed.

Palmer nodded grimly. "Yes, it was Mr. Nulin. I didn't know it at the time, of course. I gave chase for about two blocks before he slipped into a back alley. I radioed the station to report the occurrence and request backup. Though I knew to wait for backup to arrive, I followed him in. That's when the fun started.

"It was really dark, and I couldn't see a thing, let alone the suspect. There were several doors, at least a dozen, running up and down the sides of the alley. Each door led to a different store in this weirdly constructed strip mall. I knew he had gone in one, but I couldn't be sure which one. Assuming he wouldn't stay near the front, I started at the back. At the last door at the end of the alley, I had a premonition then that this was where the man was. And that if I were smart, I would leave now and forget I ever saw him. It was a creepy feeling.

"I hesitated before pushing the door open. I could smell something burning. Incense, I thought. I entered slowly. It was even darker in the storeroom than in the alley. I looked around the general area, but didn't see the suspect. I was about to leave when I heard feet scurrying in the back corner of the room. Later, I surmised he made the noise for my benefit so I wouldn't leave.

"I moved silently toward the sound, careful not to make any noise myself. I didn't want him to get the upper hand by locating me." Harrison had never heard the entire story of that day and it fascinated him.

"That's when the lights came on. I crouched down below eye level. A shot rang out, striking the ground four feet or so from where I was. He had known my position the entire time. He had been toying with me," Palmer said.

"That's when he called out. *Come out. I already know where you are.* He spoke in an eerie singsong voice. Somehow, I knew he wasn't pretending. I stepped out from behind a row of boxes, prepared to fight. He was already waiting in the open when I emerged. He had this cocky smile on his face; he was so sure of himself. He walked right up to me, right in my face. He threw his gun to the side and held out his hands. He grinned and said *Congratulations. You win.*

"I stepped forward cautiously, unsure of his intentions. That's when he began to mock me. He withdrew his hands and began spouting away. *What's the matter? Here I am, the criminal, turning myself in.* He rolled his eyes and I interrupted. I asked him, *Why are you turning yourself in?*

"And do you know what he said? He said, *For the good of mankind.* I wanted so much to smack that bastard across the face for his crime and his attitude. But I didn't." Palmer sighed, partly wishing he had not held his temper that day.

"Instead, I arrested him. Read him his rights and cuffed him. He didn't resist at all. The entire time he had this strange look on his face. I dragged him out into the street. Backup had arrived seconds earlier. They were preparing to set up a blockade. I told them not to bother, I had apprehended the suspect. It surprised them I was able to catch him. You see, he was the leader of a cult. A supposed black magic cult.

"The story went that his followers kept him well sheltered from the long arm of the law. We transported him down to the station and threw him in a holding cell. He didn't want his one telephone call. Not only that, he confessed! Not just to the murders of that afternoon, but to a whole string of murders in the area. A total of thirty.

"Peter Nulin went to trial and was found guilty. He was sentenced to the chair, as you know, for the murders of that afternoon. They electrocuted him about a month ago. He always swore he would get revenge for his death, not just on me, but all of society. Now you know everything."

Harrison nodded, but still looked perplexed. "What about taking the evidence? You haven't explained that yet," he corrected Palmer.

"Ah, that's true. I guess you don't know everything."

Palmer regarded his friend. "Please don't think I'm imagining the things I'm about to tell you."

"I'll have an open mind, I can promise that much," Harrison said.

Palmer prepared to finish his story. At the exact moment he opened his mouth to speak, the walls caved in. He dove under his desk to avoid being hit as chunks of hard, crumbly rock and concrete showered down on the office. Harrison, unable to take cover, dropped to the floor in a fetal position, covering his head with his hands.

Moments later, the cave-in ended. A cloud of dust enveloped the office. Workers in the outer office scrambled around trying to pull away the pieces of wall and ceiling. As the dust settled, they could hear a faint sound from amidst the rubble and debris. A sigh of relief came from the gathered crowd surrounding the office. A rescue team pushed its way through the crowd and reached the mess.

After pulling off the rubble, they removed Harrison's body. He wasn't breathing and his pulse was faint. On the other side of the small room, Palmer crawled out from under the desk which had somehow not fallen in on him. He coughed from the dust, then noticed his partner's body. "Is he going to be alright?" he asked, worry etched on his face.

The Emergency Medical Service crew prepared the body for transport to the hospital. At Palmer's question, one of them looked over and replied, "He's stable, but we need to take him to the hospital now." The team headed for the elevator. One technician came over to check on Palmer and he shooed her away. She left with the others.

Palmer felt a stab of pain in his chest and wondered if he should have let someone examine him. He felt something hard when he placed his hand on his chest. Reaching into the hidden pocket inside his jacket, he removed… the letter and the CD. He did not remember placing them there during the turmoil. He returned both items to his pocket and walked over to the officer who seemed to be in charge.

"Hey, Max, what caused this?" he asked, glancing around the room.

Max looked up from his notes at Palmer. He appeared troubled. "I'll be damned if I know," he confessed to him. "We can't find the cause. It's like magic or something. I'll let you know as soon as I know anything."

Palmer thanked him and headed for his car with Max's comment ringing in his ears. *It's like magic.* Palmer sat for a moment before turning the key in the ignition. He placed the CD in the player and pressed play, not bothering to be careful. First there was silence; then a low raspy voice spoke. A very melodious voice, yet Palmer thought he detected a touch of something else. Nervousness, perhaps. But why should the voice be nervous? Didn't he hold all the cards?

"Come on, I know you have at least half a brain," the

CD had begun. "I've given you a major clue and you still can't figure it out." The voice sounded exasperated. "This is my final message to you. Meet me at the scene of the original crime in one hour. Come alone." The CD stopped.

Exactly one hour later, Palmer reached the office building where his original showdown with Peter Nulin took place. He figured he'd regret not telling anyone where he was, but too late now.

Armed with only a .45, he entered the darkened suite of offices into the large central office where the underlings and secretaries worked. *Déjà vu*, he thought, his mind traveling back to his first meeting with this man. If it was Peter Nulin, and not some copycat killer.

Just as before, shortly after entering, the lights came on. Palmer's eyes adjusted to the new light. He found himself in a room with only one other visible occupant. Victoria.

Bound at the wrists and ankles, she hung from the ceiling. Palmer felt sick before he realized she wasn't dead. Hanging in such a way that the rope exerted pressure around her waist, not her neck, she was just unconscious. He stepped forward.

A large cabinet stood in the middle of the room, behind where Victoria hung. From out behind this cabinet stepped a man dressed all in black, holding a gun, and emanating an almost palpable energy.

Michael Palmer called out to this man who looked an

awful lot like Peter Nulin. "Throw down your weapon, you are under arrest for kidnapping."

The man threw the gun towards Palmer, but it disappeared in a small explosion before reaching him.

"Nice trick," Palmer responded drily. "Who are you?"

A Cheshire cat smile. "Who do you think I am?"

Sobbing filled the room; Victoria had revived. Fixing her red and watery eyes on the mystery man, she cried out in surprise. "I know you. You worked for Mr. Borr." Her eyes widened with fear as she realized he was her kidnapper. Yet, she looked confused, unsure of her surroundings or the situation.

Palmer realized what had happened that day of the murders. "You killed them. Why didn't I see it before?" He questioned himself. "Now I know what didn't make sense about the case. Most of the workers questioned said there were three men with Victoria at the time of the murders. Yet, no one could remember the name of that third man, and the officers only found two heads, not three, so we thought they were mistaken. You were the third man." Palmer knew he was right, but many questions remained unanswered.

The man clapped. "Nicely done, Michael. How are you going to prove it? And that still doesn't answer the question of my identity. If I am Peter Nulin, how will you explain that a dead man did it?"

Palmer frowned. "I don't know that you are Nulin.

Why did you want the case solved?" he asked, changing the subject.

"What?"

"On the CD, you implied you wanted the case solved. Why?"

"Simple. To kill you for interfering years ago."

"Oh. I guess that answers that." He shrugged. "But if you are Nulin, why did you turn yourself in back then?"

"That incarnation bored me. It had become burdensome, what with the publicity my group was receiving. I didn't just want to disappear though. I wanted to go out with a flourish."

"So you murdered thirty people?

"Yes. I would've continued, but you had seen me. I could've avoided capture and killed some more, but it wasn't worth the effort to elude your pursuit."

"Why didn't you kill me? Then you could have continued your fun," Palmer responded sarcastically.

"I decided that taking revenge on you after you believed I was gone would be much more interesting. Besides, being electrocuted allowed the perfect way to leave my life unencumbered and with no expectations of ever being seen again. If only it hadn't taken so long to be killed," he complained, only half joking. "What an incredibly inefficient system of punishment you Americans have."

"Sorry you weren't impressed," Palmer retorted. "If you are Nulin, how did you survive? I mean, they electrocuted you, for God's sake! You said so yourself. Reincarnation, I suppose."

The man laughed. "You didn't electrocute me, only my body. Don't look at me that way. I'll explain it to you," Nulin spoke as if to a child. "My true self is a spirit of the underworld, as you mortals put it. I rule over the so-called black magic in your pitiful world. I have been around forever and cannot die. It is an impossibility."

Palmer absorbed this before replying. "Why frame Victoria? How is she involved?" In response, the spirit pointed to the door behind Palmer. Nulin never moved as the door shut and locked.

"I wasn't trying to frame her. I used the murders as a diversion." Nulin ignored the confusion apparent on Palmer's face and pointed at Victoria. Palmer watched her drop in a heap on the floor. The spirit stared at her in sudden fear. Victoria looked up, smiling.

"You thought you were so smart, burying my own memories in this mind. I will defeat you yet," she promised.

The spirit laughed, the earlier flash of fear gone. "I find your threat infantile. You are much more fun this way than as a scared hostage, however," he admitted.

Victoria stood, hands on hips, and glared at the spirit. "You cannot win against me. The power of goodness has always prevailed. I shall, again, beat you." She flung the other spirit to fly into the wall behind him.

Palmer hid behind the cabinet. *Power of goodness? Black magic? This is unreal*, he thought to himself. Although Victoria's existence as some sort of nemesis to Nulin explained the nervousness Palmer thought he had detected on the second CD. Nulin must have realized Victoria could regain her memories sooner than he expected. Palmer peered out from behind the cabinet to watch the clash between the two figures.

Victoria threw Nulin up against the wall again through sheer force of will. Angry, he tossed her into the ceiling. After a few minutes of this, neither touching the other, Victoria drew a sparkling circle on the wall behind Nulin without his apparent knowledge. She danced around the room until she had positioned herself across from the circle. Nulin had his back to the circle and remained unaware of its existence.

"Time for a long rest," Victoria whispered, and pushed the evil spirit into the middle of the circle. His eyes filled with surprise, then fear. There flashed a brief, blinding light and when it vanished, the spirits went with it. All that remained were two empty, dead bodies.

Palmer called the station to report the incident. He sat down and sighed, correctly assuming the case would go unsolved and he would have some explaining to do. He wondered if it were finally over.

Close enough to over, a voice in his head answered. It sounded like Victoria. *Do not worry*, she said. *I've taken care of everything. He is trapped, at least for several centuries, and will not return to earth in that time.*

"What happened?" Palmer asked the air, aware of the inadequacy of the question.

The voice in his head attempted to answer. *I have been following the entity you knew as Peter Nulin for decades. He usually senses my approach before I reach him. This time, he missed my presence, but I mistook Borr for him. I discovered my mistake when I went into Borr's office and saw Nulin standing next to him. I was too late. Nulin killed the other men and while I tried to fix the damage, he snuck past my defenses and pushed my identity beneath the fake Victoria I had created. Luckily, he had only the power to deter me temporarily. His obsession with revenge against you allowed me to amass my strength and defeat him. For that, I am grateful.*

"You're welcome," Palmer replied, glad he indirectly helped, but disconcerted that he had been sort of... well, bait.

Goodbye, Michael Palmer. He gave a barely perceptible nod of his head and remained sitting there.

The circle on the wall dissipated. Palmer rose to his feet and walked to the exit. Outside, laughter filled the night. *You haven't seen the last of me.*

Falling

Walking outside of her quaint Victorian house with the stereotypical suburban white picket fence, Rachel noticed a putrid smell permeating the greenish atmosphere around her. Green? The color of the air was no less odd than the ruins surrounding her. She didn't understand what had happened, or why her house still stood. Pivoting, Rachel discovered her house did not still stand; only the room she had just left remained intact. As she watched, it crumpled to the ground, like a bug smashed by a giant hand.

Unbidden, concern crept into Rachel's mind that she might be the only person left alive on the planet. She felt immeasurable relief when she heard a minute noise behind her. *Someone else is alive, too.* She turned toward the sound smiling, not considering what may confront her. Eyes wide, the color draining from her face, she began mumbling disjointedly.

What she saw before her once had been human. However, the one-armed creature bore only the slightest resemblance to humans now. Rachel's eyes traveled from the three-fingered hand, up the torn and bruised arm to the hideously misshapen face of the creature standing before her. She stared in horror, frozen, while the creature spoke to her again before it fell face first into the debris. Not understanding the creature and scared by its appearance, Rachel screamed and sobbed. She finally collapsed to the ground in shock.

From the air behind her, a hand with only four fingers reached out and gripped Rachel's shoulder. It gripped so strong she could not pull free. She fainted as the trauma of everything crashed down upon her.

Rachel awoke in a dark room unable to see her own hand mere inches before her face. Quivering uncontrollably, she yelled and screamed until she was hoarse.

A blinding light filled the room the instant her screams ceased. The intensity seared Rachel's body. Her eyes snapped shut while her hands futilely attempted to shield her face from the onslaught.

Rachel must have slept then, because her next conscious experience was in a different room, surrounded by multiple alien creatures. They appeared to be humans, except for the minor discrepancies of missing a nose, one eye, and one finger off each hand.

Oddly enough, Rachel felt numb, not scared, though she expected to faint again. Ten of the creatures milled around the room. She shrank back in horror when they approached. Two of them grabbed her arms while a third injected a syringe filled with a foreign substance into the fleshy part of her upper arm. The substance bubbled and glowed, burning as it entered her body.

Rachel fell in a never-ending pit of multi-colored scaly walls and charred floating bones. She heard people comforting her, but she recognized the facade. The knowledge that death approached filled her with fear. She cried for her mom and dad, her best friend Jenny, and for the stuffed animals that used to fill her demolished bedroom.

Rachel was falling and falling into a new world in another dimension, yet she knew she would never reach her destination. She would just continue falling and falling and falling...

"Poor Rachel. So unfortunate. Do they know what happened?" Mrs. Laver asked her husband.

"The rumor is that the hospital found heroin in her bloodstream. They believe she was high as a kite on that trash when she went up on the roof, and suspect that's what caused her to fall, or jump. Nothing's been confirmed yet. I feel so bad for her family. Such a tragedy," he replied, his voice filled with

remorse for the dead girl and her family. "Did you know she'd been struggling with a heroin addiction?"

"My goodness, no," answered his wife. "And only 16."

…falling and falling forever, for all of eternity. Confusion and disorientation consumed her. She tired of the discomfort, craved oblivion that did not come. Rachel traveled through time and space, falling and falling and falling and…

Conversation with Myself

A heaviness lays in my being, an emptiness in my heart.
The city around me a parasite sucking
the happiness,
the laughter,
the joy
from my life.

I wonder sometimes what would happen if I left.
Not just the city, but life.
If I simply ceased to exist, was plucked out of the picture.

Would anybody care?
Would anybody even notice I was gone?
A terrible fear grips me when I think of such questions,
because I know the answer is always going to be no.
If I dropped out of existence today
it would be but a minor setback.

For I am only one cog in the machine
among many virtually indistinguishable cogs.
A new one would be easily found
to fulfill my obligations and purpose in the world.

So forlorn.
Why is it this way?
Is it the city, crushing me with its weight
of desolation,
isolation,
desecration?
As I sit alone in my tiny room, my cell for the future,
I ponder the infinite questions and gaze,
not quite serenely,
into the depths of despair, and ask
Is it worth it?

I dissect an answerable question into its tiny unanswerable
bits and pieces.
What is it?
Life, the city, my job, my future?
What is worth?
Desire, need, price, justification?
And again, what is it?
Pain, isolation, depression, oppression?

Who knows the answers to these questions
that cause my brain to spin
and my eyes and head to ache?

I certainly do not, as I sit
on my hard, carpeted floor,
scribbling this by lamplight
on an overcast, rainy day

in the City That Never Sleeps.
My confused brain accepts that I shall endure
this city,
its evils,
and crushing apathy
for only a while longer.

Will I be happy when I leave,
or will these
questions,
ponderings,
utterances
follow me wherever I go,
dooming me to a life of suffering and inner turmoil?

I desperately wish that will not be the case.
That when I leave this city and this job,
I will be reborn into the world
and nevermore wonder if anyone would notice or care
if I ceased to exist in the morning.

Dream within a Dream

Have you ever pondered the meaning of your existence? It's hard enough in the corporeal realm; but, man, here it's nearly... wait. Before I ramble on with existential questions about the meaning of life and death, perhaps I should start at the beginning. The first thing I became aware of was sound. Somebody moving around my room. I opened my eyes.

"Where am I?"

A man in the bland white room faced me. "Alison, you're in the hospital," the man, a doctor or nurse I assumed, explained. He held a needle, which alarmed me, as did his futile attempt to soothe my nervousness.

"I'm Nurse Landers. I've been caring for you. I promise the needle won't hurt much. It's a mild sedative to help you remain calm." His small smile didn't quite meet his brown eyes.

"Why do I need a shot to remain calm? I just woke up." I didn't much care for being drugged immediately upon waking up, and I guessed my tone of voice reflected that.

Nurse Landers ran his hand though his curly brown hair. "You see, Alison. Look how upset you are. This will just reduce your anxiety," he said, indicating the sedative. I offered my arm despite my confusion and anger.

After the nurse administered the drug, I drifted to sleep, but not a restful sleep. Instead, I dreamed.

A circular table with three occupied seats was the focal point of a brightly lit room. In each chair sat a replica of me. Except that the ones on either side differed radically from each other, and only one was truly identical to me.

The first one wore a short, tight mini-dress, fishnet stockings, and stiletto heels. Before her on the table sat a little gold card with the name Ruby printed on it. The girl to Ruby's left looked physically to be about nineteen, the same as the others, but her outfit contradicted that age. Dressed like an infant, complete with a diaper, she wore a pink bonnet over blond baby doll curls. Her gold plaque read Kaitlin.

The final of the three appeared conspicuous in her normality. She looked just as I vaguely remembered I did when I wasn't in the hospital, dressed in a clean, essentially fashionable outfit. She had a plaque with black lettering that read Melissa.

These three versions of me sat around the table staring at, and talking to, a small snake. The snake appeared to comprehend the girls' spoken words and responded nonverbally. At first, the girls' words were too faint to be decipherable, but gradually became clear.

"What are we gonna do?" whined Kaitlin.

"Be quiet," responded Ruby. "Let's hear what Melissa has to say." Her tone established who was the woman in charge.

Melissa's eyes remained fixed on those of the snake, a malicious grin on her face. At her name, the expression disappeared and she looked up at the young women seated beside her.

"There is nothing to be done," she stated in a monotone. "The serpent maintains total control. At the start of..." The voice tapered off until it was inaudible.

"Alison?" The softly spoken word pulled me out of the dream. I opened my eyes to find the gentle face of Nurse Landers staring back at me. I somehow knew something was wrong and, hating to ask, did anyway.

"What's the matter? What's wrong?"

"Nothing's wrong. Everything is normal," Nurse Landers said, his words sounding false.

Anger welled up inside at the nurse's deliberate evasiveness or even outright lying. I wouldn't be here if nothing was wrong. But, I didn't feel sick. I'd had enough with this hospital and this nurse, who hardly looked old enough to be practicing medicine. And I still didn't even know why I was there. Were all hospitals run this way?

I struggled to sit up, fighting the continued heady effect of the sedative. Once able to sit up, I glowered at Nurse Landers. It required quite an effort.

"I have had enough. I've been given drugs and treated like I have a terminal case of... something, with no explanation." My irritation intensified when I realized my words sounded slurred. "I want to know exactly why I am here. I want to know what is going on and where my family is. Enough is enough." I was shaking, my fists clenched at my sides, trying not to fall over in the bed. I wanted answers and, unfortunately, my fuzzy brain could recall nothing from the recent past.

"What do you remember, Alison?"

"Nothing," I snapped. Nausea hit me. A memory returned. "I was at home arguing with my sister about the menu for a party we were planning for, um, a time in the future. I was yelling at her, screaming, actually, when I felt something..."

"What did you feel?"

"The weirdest thing. An almost physical sensation of something growing inside of me." I frowned, searching the memory. "My eyes focused on the counter for a long while – and a knife lying there," I added offhandedly, "and then everything went black." I shrugged. "The next thing I remember is waking up here. Which hospital is this, anyway? County General?"

Pain engulfed my head causing a gasp that preempted the nurse's answer. I grabbed the sides of my head, shrieking, slamming my body from side to side, the pain unbearable. The pain subsided slightly. I moaned, then stopped and was silent.

At my initial screaming, a guard rushed in, gun drawn.

"Are you okay? What happened?" the officer asked, crossing to the bed. Was the question directed at me or the nurse? I never thought to wonder why there would be a guard so close to my room. Instead, I passed out.

Psychedelic lights and sounds surrounded me. The sounds beat in time to the sound of my heart. Quick and irregular. My skin seemed to melt into the pulsing light, becoming translucent. I saw my blood flowing in my veins, saw my cells divide and multiply, divide and multiply.

Something had heightened my senses so much that I could not only see the lights, but feel them deep in my bones. Gradually the friendly atmosphere ebbed away to a dark and foreboding one. I had already become indistinguishable from the air around me and sharp fear made my teeth chatter. The dark light swirled and shifted until there appeared before me a black hole. From the back of the hole, a shape emerged. My body shook with anxiety as the shape drew closer.

The object took on the recognizable form of a serpent, but it was extraordinary. An acrid evil odor overwhelmed my senses. The stench shrouded the serpent like the smoke around a burning building. Along with the horrendous smell, it emitted atrocious sounds reminiscent of nails dragged down a chalkboard, but multiplied infinitely. The sound filled the cavity in which I resided. It pulsated around the room, reverberating off the walls, increasing the decibel level higher and higher until I felt positive my eardrums would burst.

After the assault on my nose and ears, the serpent's appearance was almost benign. Wide eyes, unnaturally wide. They seemed peaceful, but I sensed fanatical madness lurking just below the surface. It had a pale line of a mouth beneath the eyes. Black scales of a symmetrical design covered the face and body.

Not born of my world, the serpent looked to be straight out of hell. It radiated an almost palpable evil. The serpent opened its mouth a fraction of an inch wide and spoke, in a voice remarkably similar to my own. Its words were articulate and slow, the serpent taking the time to form them perfectly. Raspy at first, the voice became clearer as it progressed.

"Hello, Alison. You know who I am – or maybe you aren't aware of me – but we have yet to be formally introduced." *The serpent sounded female.*

"I am Melissa, one of your other selves," *she explained in a melodious voice.* "I am the strongest of all of your 'inner selves'." *A slight sneer accompanied the last comment. Her voice turned hard as steel, and just as cold.*

"I am taking control, and there is nothing you can do to stop me. This carcass is useless to you now; or to me when I emerge. Therefore, I will leave it behind when I join your world permanently. As for you, well, let's just say it's not a concern of yours anymore."

Unbelieving, I stared at the serpent, thinking, What an odd dream. *I wondered whether the earlier drugs they had given me could conjure up something so diabolical and twisted. I almost believed it wasn't real. Slowly disbelief changed to horror.*

"Wait a minute. If you're part of me, then how can you leave my physical body behind? And where are you coming from if you aren't part of my world?"

"I originated from what your world refers to as a parallel universe. We occupy the same space, and yet we don't. Your world considers us repulsive; an intelligent, reptilian life form. However, my species considers itself infinitely superior to yours. This is why we have never made contact before. I, however, was given no choice. My world no longer has war, hunger, poverty, or any of the other societal ills that delightfully seem to plague your planet." *The snake paused for a breath.*

"Why have you come here? Why were you given no choice?" *I asked, confused by the serpent's explanation. How could she be part of me, yet not of my world? And what did that mean for the other selves she mentioned?*

Before the serpent could finish responding to my surprisingly lucid (I thought) questions, a mysterious black surrounded me.

There flashed a brief surge of light, which recurred

stronger and stronger until it steadied and I was aware of voices. I woke up that way often it seemed. I was indeed waking up as the narcotic wore off.

The voices belonged to Nurse Landers and Dr. Kozy (at least that's what the nurse called her). She was reviewing a chart as I woke, presumably mine.

Dr. Kozy smiled and walked over. I eyed her warily. Almost unaware of my doing so, I watched from outside my body as I lurched forward, clawing at her face. Dr. Kozy lost her smile and wrestled with my abnormally strong body. I remember thinking, *who is controlling it if I'm out here?* I felt trapped in an old episode of *Twin Peaks* or *The Twilight Zone*.

Dr. Kozy yelled for additional nurses to restrain me, while Nurse Landers prepared another needle of the sedative. Before he could inject it, my body had clawed everyone in the room, giving them deep gashes on their faces and hands. The body screamed about how she would get them all as the medicine worked through her system. It was all very surreal.

It was dark, the darkness as thick as an inexplicable nighttime fog. Then it was bright, so bright my eyes hurt. The source was a single ray of light, illuminating me. In a cage. Darkness swirled and shifted as before and the black hole appeared. The serpent again emerged from the hole. Different from the first dream; larger, much larger. The serpent wrapped itself (herself?) around the cage. I was in a kind of catatonic state. At least, my body would not respond to any demands for movement. My eyes were wide and vacant; I could not focus or look side to side.

Hissing, the serpent squeezed the cage. As it crushed my body to death, the serpent spoke. Perhaps it felt some need to continue its explanation to the life it was seizing. "I have begun. You asked why I was here. My kind banished me from my home. I was ostracized for being different. Violent where others were peaceful, argumentative where others were compliant. Through your world, so different from mine, yet so like me, I will exact my revenge. After I have built up my strength with the anger and negativity of your world, I will return to my own place and time. And destroy all who would deny me."

I heard my voice filtered weakly through the sound of crushing bars. "Why me?" *It was all I could say. By appearances, I was vegetative, but I knew my body was dying, and the question was all I could find the energy to utter. My mind, however, was hyperactive, screaming out questions. What would happen to me?*

"Why you? Why indeed. You were open at the right place at the right time. You already had a weak mind. I just filled in the empty spaces your fractured personality created inside of you. You are quite insane. Do you remember how you killed your own sister? You hacked Elizabeth to pieces and cut off your father's arm when he tried to stop you. All this turmoil caused your mother to have a nervous breakdown. She's on so much medication, the only action she can perform is to drool out of the corner of her mouth." *The snake chuckled at the vision.* "Although, to remain truthful, you didn't really do any of it. I killed your sister and destroyed your family. You probably could have taken drugs that would have made you normal. Well, no matter, you won't suffer much longer." *The light faded to complete black, along with any sense of physical being.*

Whatever happened to Melissa, Kaitlyn, and Ruby? Or Alison, for that matter? I don't know. On to other questions. You may wonder how I could tell my story if I'm dead. I often wonder where I am, who I am. Clearly, I exist with some level of awareness – so am I dead or living? Is this heaven or hell, or another form of existence? The major question, though, that haunts me is whether I am to be this disembodied something for all time. Man, I hope not. I'd rather be truly unaware than drift for eternity in this… void.

Oh well, sweet dreams. . .

Nothing

Staring into the abyss
There is nothing.

Such a terribly long way
Down to nothing.

A bleak, dismal view
Into the heart of nothing.

A reflection of my soul –
I, too, am nothing.

Inside the Ant Farm

"I used to be normal," Linda muttered in frustration. "Go away." The image before her ignored the request, so she resolutely shut her eyes. "When I count to ten, everything will be the way it's supposed to be." Counting upward, she dreaded reaching ten, for fear the image would remain. At last, she opened her eyes.

"Thank goodness," she breathed in a sigh of relief. The wall of her apartment was just a wall again. Gone were the teeming creatures she had seen instead of the smooth white plaster.

Scribbling in her journal that night, Linda contemplated the last few days. The hallucinations had begun with no warning. As she sat in her lecture class for freshman English, the blackboard behind her professor had become translucent. She'd managed not to show her surprise; growing up in a family of gamblers had taught her how to keep an excellent poker face. However, she had expected at least one of the other hundred and thirty-eight souls in the room to react to the change. But, glancing around, she had observed no sharp intake of breath, eyes wide in surprise, or a simmering of voices chattering excitedly. Nobody had noticed. Or nothing had happened to notice. It was this last thought that stuck in Linda's mind. If no one else could see the disturbance, obviously it wasn't real. Right?

For the rest of the week, the occurrences continued at least a couple per day. Linda was at a loss for what to do. She did not want to tell her parents, who would definitely pressure her to quit school. She also didn't want to tell anyone even remotely connected to the school; they might decide she was unfit to continue. Since the images hadn't interfered yet, she decided to ignore them.

Until dreams that she couldn't remember upon awakening began completely disrupting her sleep patterns.

Linda went to the university health clinic for some sleeping pills, hoping to get at least a decent night's rest. Big mistake. Sure, she slept like a baby, but the next day the hallucinations hit with a vengeance.

Staring into the mirror that morning, Linda wondered if her lack of sleep caused the dark circles under her eyes or if she could blame the stress of the hallucinations. As if on cue, her face in the mirror appeared to melt as the reflective surface altered. Linda found herself peering through, in effect, a window into another world. She stared in fascination at the beings on the other side moving around a white room filled with plastic and metal objects. She didn't recognize the creatures or their equipment. She briefly wondered if she was insane or looking through a portal to another universe.

Linda studied the beings while they bustled back and forth. They bore a striking resemblance to the creatures in everyday alien abduction stories. Gray humanoids, no ears, with large luminous black eyes. *My hallucination is a stereotype of the aliens next door. How trite,* she thought to herself, chuckling. The scene dragged on and on, with no change. Just as she was ready to turn from the scene in boredom, the mirror became a mirror again.

The sight of her own wide blue eyes in a pale face staring back at her startled Linda out of the semi-trance into which she had fallen.

"Damn, that was so realistic," she explained to herself in the mirror. "I never realized hallucinations could be so realistic." Turning from the mirror, the time on her nightstand clock shocked her. "I don't believe it!" She grabbed her books and slipped on a pair of sandals. The interlude of conversing with herself had capped an apparent hour spent staring at the scene in the mirror. "I'm beginning to feel like a character in a science fiction novel," she muttered aloud as she slammed out of the front door to her apartment.

"How nice of you to join us," Dr. Collins commented dryly as Linda rushed into the classroom.

"I'm sorry I'm late. I lost track of time this morning," Linda explained, silently cursing her luck. Her twice weekly freshman seminar course would be the class she was late for, since it only had fifteen people in it and her absence impossible to miss.

"We were just discussing last night's reading. What did you think?" Linda dumped her stuff in a pile at her chair and tried to compose her thoughts before answering.

An hour later, Linda wandered around campus, trying to make sense of her morning vision. Unfortunately, she returned again and again to the conclusion she was crazy. She didn't feel crazy, but wondered if the crazy person was the last to know. She decided not to take the sleeping pill that night. Whether that was a mistake or not would depend on your point of view of the events that transpired.

Linda tossed fitfully in bed; then the dream started. She stood in the room she had observed in the mirror. Only this time, she was right in the middle of everything. She wandered around, trying to determine her exact location. The creatures worked around her, not noticing her presence. Linda didn't like being ignored, plus she really wanted to know what was going on, so she walked up to one of the creatures.

"Hey, there. I have a couple of questions about this little gig you've got going here," Linda started, just as the creature walked through her. "Whoa, that was weird," she exhaled in a rush. Evidently, she was invisible. As an experiment, she tried to pick up a few things sitting on the counters. She felt the presence of something that physically existed, but her fingers went right through it all. Stepping toward a corner, she observed the actions of the creatures.

Based on the beakers and test tubes and fancy equipment she could now see, Linda surmised she was in a lab. But she couldn't figure out what they were doing. At one point she observed what looked like excited chatter among the creatures, though she couldn't identify the cause.

A loud buzzing filled Linda's ears, but the creatures appeared unaffected. As the scene around her faded, she realized the noise came from her alarm clock.

Linda smacked the clock with her palm, sat up and yawned. *What an odd dream!* She shook her head to clear out the cobwebs of sleep, then stood. She wondered when the hallucinations would begin for the day. They never did that day. Or the day after that. Or the day after that. In fact, for the next week, she didn't experience a single hallucination during the day. On the other hand, her dreams remained focused on the alien laboratory. She learned nothing new about the lab, but at least her daylight hours remained free from the craziness.

Linda groaned in exasperation when the wall in the bathroom shimmered slightly. *Well, it was nice while it lasted,* she thought. She knew another hallucination was about to start. "No," she muttered under her breath, but to no avail. She stared at the all-too-familiar interior of the laboratory, the aliens scurrying back and forth. Even though she was in a restaurant bathroom, Linda had had enough. The time had come to find out who these creatures were, what they were doing, and why they were doing it to her.

"Excuse me," she whispered. "May I ask what you're doing?" Several of the creatures in the lab stopped their activity and stared straight ahead, as if hearing something they could not identify.

"I'm about to wash my hands. Why?"

Linda shook her head after one creature responded, before realizing the response came from the woman who had walked up to the sink next to her. The woman who now looked at her askance.

"I'm sorry," Linda told the woman, never taking her eyes off of the scene in front of her. "I was just talking to myself."

"Um, okay. Didn't mean to interrupt your musings." The woman gave Linda one final look and fled the facilities.

"Thanks a lot, guys, now I look like a lunatic," Linda told the creatures in the lab who had gone back to what they were working on. At the sound of her voice, they once again stopped what they were doing, more of them this time, and stared around the room. They were clearly trying to locate the source of the sound. "I said it." Several of the creatures looked toward her before turning away. "You can't see me," she said, "just hear me." The creatures gestured wildly at each other, and, in fact, a couple even left the room. Abruptly, the image faded.

"Wait, I want someone to acknowledge me," Linda cried out as the mirror became a mirror again. Looking into the eyes of the startled woman in the reflection, she sighed inwardly. Linda turned to the woman standing behind her, who appeared vaguely frightened, and gave the woman a lopsided grin. "I'm rehearsing my lines for a play I'm doing."

The woman visibly relaxed. "Of course you are," she immediately agreed. Linda smiled and nodded, then made her way to the door. "Break a leg," the woman called after her as the door began to close.

Linda rolled her eyes at the entire scene while she made her way to her car parked in the restaurant parking lot. Sitting in the driver's seat, she reflected that it was a good thing she hadn't been dining with anyone tonight. That night, she slept the sleep of the dead, with no dreams she could recall the next morning.

"Maybe all I had to do to end the hallucinations and dreams was to acknowledge them," she told herself in the mirror, hugely pleased that it remained a mirror. "Maybe the whole strange episode is over now." Hoping her life might be back to normal, Linda left her apartment and got in her car to drive to campus. She immediately noticed a change.

"Where are all the people?" she wondered aloud as her lone car sped up the road. There wasn't a single other person on the road with her. No matter what time of the day, especially on a college campus, someone was awake and driving somewhere. Linda's uneasiness increased once she reached campus. She saw no one, not a student, worker, or professor, from the point she entered the campus until she parked her car in an outlying lot. Everything looked normal. All the buildings remained standing and other cars parked in the lot besides hers, but no other people.

That was when she registered the absolute quiet of the world around her. No car noises, no people talking, no birds, no anything. The world was still. Feeling like the world's biggest idiot (and its only idiot, she feared), Linda hollered.

"Hello! Is anybody else here? Hello?" She waited for a response, her apprehension growing by leaps and bounds. "Hello! Can anybody hear me? If you can hear me, please say something," Linda shouted into the stillness, noting the edge of hysteria in her voice. Losing it now would not help her discover what had happened.

"Quit yelling. I can hear you," came a quiet voice from behind Linda. Relief flooded through her body at the sound and she turned toward the voice.

"Oh, thank goodness. You wouldn't believe the scenario I was..." She fell silent once facing the source of the voice. A gray creature stood before her.

"What the hell is going on here? Are you another hallucination or am I dreaming?" Linda demanded, having decided righteous indignation was preferable to sheer terror.

"Neither, actually." The alien appeared to have a mouth, yet Linda would have sworn it communicated telepathically. She wasn't hearing words so much as she was accepting them.

"What are you, then?"

"I am what you would call an alien."

"Of course," Linda muttered, slapping her open hand against her forehead with a little overdone theatrics. "Do you come in peace or is this the start of an invasion?" She meant the question as a joke, but the alien regarded her quizzically for a moment before responding with all seriousness.

"Neither. We already control your world. Why would we now invade it?"

The alien asked as if confused, but Linda suspected a ruse. The alien had to be aware of what its appearance meant; to her and the planet. "Cut the crap and let me in on the plan," Linda snapped, her previous anger boiling just below the surface of her words.

"They sent me to fix you."

"To fix me? I'm not broken. What are you talking about?" Some fear crept back, fighting with the anger for space in her mind.

"You have been seeing images that shouldn't be there," the alien persisted.

"Yes. So?"

"That shouldn't happen. I'm here to make sure it doesn't."

"How?"

"I will fix your brain pattern."

"That's okay, my brain pattern is fine," Linda assured the alien while backing away slowly. Cocking her head to one side, she paused in her retreat. "How do you know English so well?"

"I don't. Your brain can interpret what I am… saying… and translate it into a form you understand."

"Oh." Linda thought for a moment. "Wait, you never answered my question and now I have another one. Where is everybody? What are you – not you the individual, but you the alien race – doing here? Why would I have problems with my brain pattern that require fixing?"

"Since you won't remember this conversation later, I guess there's no harm in telling you," the alien conceded. "To your question, the people are all around you."

"I don't see anyone."

"No, because we are out of step with the universe."

"What?"

"I can't explain it in a way you'll understand any better than that."

"Fine. Continue then."

"I will continue, but do not interrupt with questions. Wait until I am finished," the alien admonished Linda. She nodded her head in mute agreement. "Earth is an experiment, analogous to one of your ant farms. When we first came to this rock two thousand years ago, humans were nothing, a blot on the surface. You were the perfect beginning phase – almost an empty slate.

"At first we believed we could run our experiment through interspecies breeding. The artificially created offspring of that union was a hybrid your society called Jesus. He acutely felt his difference from the people around him and that opened him in ways we did not anticipate. He was exalted among your kind and tried to push your society toward the greater good. But the evil was too great and they killed him. It was an excellent idea, interspecies breeding, but too many results like Jesus and the experiment would fail.

"We decided the experiment would have to proceed differently. We developed a biological computer chip and implanted it in millions of humans around the world. This chip contains a unique signature, or radio tag, and is passed along in the genetic material of the offspring of the original subjects. We have complete access to and control of the minds that possess a chip. We set events in motion to see how humans will respond, and, at other times, we take full control so you respond how we choose. Questions?"

"Questions?" Linda repeated back in a daze. She shook her head as if to knock out the chip that might be nestled in there; a biological stowaway, invader. "When you fix someone, you do something to the chip?"

"Yes. Occasionally, and more frequently lately, the chips malfunction or cease to work at all. In your case, the chip linked to us somehow. That has never happened before – which is why I wanted to talk to you before I fixed your brain pattern. Usually, people just have nightmares that they do not remember upon waking. When that happens, we lose control over that human. We abduct those humans and fix them."

"This is disgusting. Don't you have a Prime Directive or something?" Linda spat the words at the alien, who looked perplexed a moment before he evidently made the *Star Trek* connection.

"Your species experiments on lesser life forms all the time. You even eat them. How is what we do any different, except that this time the humans are the recipients?" The alien didn't ask the question to justify its actions, but out of what appeared to be genuine curiosity. Linda, however, took the question the former way.

"First of all, not everyone eats the flesh of other creatures. In fact, every year, more and more people recognize it as wrong. Second, the same could be said of experimentation. We explore alternatives that, slowly but surely, companies adopt. You see, we are an evolving, learning species," Linda finished passionately. Her expression changed as if tasting something sour. "Unless, even in that regard, we've been puppets on a string."

"No," the alien assured her. "Mostly, we simply observe natural life. Or we cause an event and observe the results. We rarely orchestrate reaction in the human subjects."

"Doesn't matter," Linda told the alien, shaking her head. "It isn't right to manipulate others. Even lesser life forms," she acknowledged with slight sarcasm. "I would have thought an advanced species would have advanced morals as well. I guess not," she concluded.

"What would you have us do?"

"Allow the biochips to malfunction completely. Eventually, they'll be left behind as just more pieces of genetic flotsam. When all traces of your interference are gone, come back and establish true contact with my world. You can learn a lot more by interacting with us, rather than observing," Linda proposed, warming to her idea.

"I will bring your proposal back to our scientists," the alien decided, and Linda's world went black...

...Linda peeked open her eyes, aware of a raging headache.

"What's going on?" Her voice sounded weak to her own ears.

"Just rest. You passed out in front of the art building and were brought here."

Linda opened her eyes completely to see a kind face staring at her with mild concern. "I passed out?"

"Yeah, took a bump on the head. You'll be fine. Though, I'd like you to stay in bed until some of your strength returns."

Linda glanced around the room, realized she was in an infirmary. "I had the weirdest dream. How long have I been out?"

"Just a few minutes; not enough to dream," the nurse said. "You must have been thinking heavy thoughts before you hit the deck." The nurse grinned at her own quip, and Linda smiled in response. "You just rest." And then the nurse left, leaving Linda alone with her thoughts.

"Was it real? Or a hallucination? Or a dream?" Linda questioned aloud. "The fact that I remember everything signifies... something. Here I go, talking to myself again," she finished with a laugh. She mused silently, *I suppose I'll never know.*

War & Death

the soldiers march by
chanting their war cries
no one can hear them
their cries of the dead
so silent in the air
drowned out completely
like warriors of old
they march in perfect step
stomp, stomp, over more dead
protecting their country
from imagined enemies
war is a rich man's toy

Illusion of Truth

"Would you look at that?" The young woman pointed to a figure on the ground. "Do you think she's dead?"

"No," her older companion replied, pointing to the empty beer cans. "She just can't hold her liquor." This comment elicited a round of laughter which woke the object of merriment.

"Hey, quit makin' noise," the girl mumbled, pulling herself to an upright position. Focusing her bleary eyes on the woman before her, she belched.

"That was beautiful, kid," the older woman declared, brushing frizzy blond hair off of her face. The drunk girl passed back out.

After sleeping for about five hours, the girl awoke sober, but with one hellacious hangover. The two strangers sat several feet away. When the girl shakily stood, they hurried to her side.

"Who are you?" she asked.

The blond spoke. "I am Iona Stolton and this," pointing to the young woman with auburn hair, "is my niece, Julia."

"Hello. Who are you?" Julia extended her hand, smiling.

Trying to shake off her hangover, the girl replied with an air of superiority. "I am Maxine Drake, daughter of Richard Drake, the owner of Drake Enterprises."

Julia regarded her with amusement. "I'm impressed," she laughed, "but what difference does it make if you were the heir to a fortune? Look around, people can take anything they want. What good is material wealth now?"

"What are you talking about? Of course, material wealth matters," Maxine replied indignantly. "Why wouldn't it?"

Iona and Julia exchanged puzzled glances. "After the war decimated the populace," Julia began, but Maxine interrupted.

"War? What war?" She looked at the world around her. It seemed normal, if messier and quieter. "Where is everybody?"

"What do you remember?" Iona asked, instead of allowing Julia to answer Maxine's questions. Maxine thought hard for a moment, then her face brightened.

With her white-blond hair, her head practically glowed in the afternoon sun.

"I was at a party when everybody started yelling and throwing stuff. I grabbed a twelve-pack and some pills and left."

"When was this?" Julia asked, already guessing the answer.

"I don't know. Do you?" Maxine asked anxiously in response.

"Yes. One week ago, today," Iona answered.

Maxine's eyes widened. "No way. Daddy would have come after me if I disappeared for that long," she insisted.

"Not if he's dead."

"Iona, really! Have some compassion," Julia reprimanded her aunt.

"My father is not dead," Maxine declared.

"You know what your problem is, kid? You don't understand the situation now and you don't know about anything important. You've spent the last week eating who knows what and staying permanently sloshed. Let me tell you how lucky you are that we found your scrawny butt!"

"It isn't necessary to be mean, Iona," Maxine sniffed. "I didn't ask to be born into a family of wealth and privilege. Did I?"

"No, but I'm sure you milked it."

"Perhaps it would be more constructive to tell Maxine what she, um, slept through," Julia interceded.

"You go ahead," Iona said with a dismissive wave.

"I assume you remember the Superiors, elected in 2050 to replace the single president?" Julia asked Maxine.

"Of course. Do I look like a moron? I'm eighteen years old, an adult, not a child."

"Right. Anyway, as you also no doubt know, this last year, 2055, almost every country possessed the ability to employ biological weapons powerful enough to wipe out most of the population of their targets. And many were threatening to do so."

"Yes, I remember the peace talks between us, the European Union, the Asian Coalition, and that Middle East group were breaking down. People were afraid World War III would happen." Understanding dawned on Maxine's face. "Is that what happened last week?"

Julia nodded sadly. "Yes. During the peace talks, something went awry. What you don't remember is that the leaders of the world, including the four Superiors, activated their weapons systems. The projected survival rate was less than 1% of the world's population. Only those with a specific genetic immunity survived. It happened too fast to stop. Most people stayed home and prayed – and their bodies are now rotting in those homes. That's why you don't see any people anywhere."

"Did everybody die?" Maxine squeaked out the question.

"No, because we are alive," Julia said. "And so are others. We were on our way to find a city with working electricity when we stumbled across you."

"I guess that makes sense, but how come electricity isn't on everywhere?" Maxine asked, in obvious confusion. Iona chuckled, but Julia patiently explained.

"There aren't enough knowledgeable people left alive in this area. For that reason, we'll camp out as we travel to a city with some electricity. You're welcome to join us," Julia offered, "but you will do your share."

"Thanks, I will," Maxine accepted, although her discomfort at *camping out* was plain. "Why don't we stay at my house for the night? Someone in my family may still be alive. In the morning, we can pack as much as we need in my father's old backpacks before heading for civilization." Iona and Julia agreed, and the three set off for Maxine's McMansion.

"They're really gone," Maxine whispered when the trio discovered the bodies of Maxine's father, mother, and sister.

"I'm sorry, Maxine," Julia offered, knowing the small comfort that would bring.

"Thank you," Maxine responded, tears overfilling her eyes. No one spoke as the three set about burying Maxine's family. They left early in the morning after a restless night.

As they walked, a rustling sound off to the right snapped Maxine out of her thoughts. The three turned to find a thing resembling a human limping around a parked car. The creature looked like it had fought a wild animal.

"What is that?" Maxine screeched. Both Julia and Iona motioned for her to be quiet. They gazed in horror while the thing approached. When within earshot, they could hear mumbling, soon forming recognizable words.

"You think I'm hard to look at," it spoke in a faint, raspy female voice. Struggling, she continued, "Wait... wait until you meet Ahriman. Already he... has a reputation." She coughed spasmodically as she walked to Maxine. "I was left alive to deliver a message. You are the chosen one." She reached out and touched Maxine's shoulder. Ignoring Maxine's blatant repulsion, the woman added, "Only you can prevent the destruction of... the world." Having completed her task, she fell dead into Maxine's arms. Maxine held her before setting the body on the ground. She faced the other women and shrugged to hide her fear.

"That was weird. She was obviously delirious from being attacked by someone," Maxine offered as an explanation.

"Maybe. It's only been a week, but there are already rumors about this Ahriman. One of them spoke of a man saving the world by stopping the beast from getting some object. Pretty vague, I know," Julia said.

"I'm not a man," Maxine pointed out.

"I know, but that part could just be a fact of living in a patriarchal society. No one would expect the world's savior to be a woman. That doesn't mean it couldn't be," Julia countered.

"We don't know that the world is in further danger," Iona interrupted. "And besides, even if it is, a rich kid with no knowledge of the world certainly isn't going to be able to save it."

Maxine stormed off as Iona chortled.

"What is your problem? If I didn't know better, I'd say you were prejudiced," Julia told her aunt.

"Me? Prejudiced? About what?" Iona seemed genuinely surprised and shocked at the accusation.

"Of what? Of people with money. You're jealous that her family had more money than we did." Iona's stunned expression hardened at the statement. Julia gave up and headed toward Maxine.

"Hey, are you okay?" Julia asked.

"What do I care what your aunt thinks of me?"

"I don't guess you would care what she thinks about you. She didn't mean anything by it, anyway. That's just her way," Julia explained.

"Just because I never wanted to camp out and learn survival skills doesn't mean I'm not smart or important. I could be a savior," Maxine stated haughtily.

"Yeah, you and Jesus," Julia responded with a smirk.

"How dare you mock me? Who do you think you are?"

Julia was about to respond when the air filled with terrible howling and wailing. Julia, Iona, and Maxine huddled together in fear. The sound rose to an unbearable pitch. Then, just as suddenly as it had begun, it stopped. No one knew what to make of it.

Iona wasted no time in taking charge. "Okay, that was weird, but it isn't important right now. We can't let odd noises frighten us. We need to find a city with electricity."

"Remember what the woman told us. Regardless of whether you think she was right, we will find this Ahriman and destroy him," Maxine declared. Julia stared at her, lost in thought.

"Are you kidding?" Iona asked. "You can go find this creature if you want to. But I will not endanger my life or my niece's over a rumor that may not even resemble the truth." She stared pointedly at Maxine. "Besides, what will you do? Boast it to death?"

This time Maxine stood her ground. "If you don't want to accompany me, that's fine, but it's Julia's decision if she wants to go. You cannot decide for her."

"Oh, yes, I can," Iona replied with finality. "She is my niece and my responsibility."

"Who says she has to do what you want? Who's going to stop her from making her own decisions? You?" Maxine sneered.

Julia stepped between the two. "Neither of you will tell me what I can or cannot do, nor what I want or do not want to do. I am my own person, so you can stop fighting over me as if I were a child. I already decided about it anyway," she added offhandedly. She turned to face her aunt.

"I'm twenty-one years old and can take care of myself. Sorry, but I'm going with Maxine. My gut tells me we should do something. I wish you would reconsider and come with us. What else are we going to do?"

Although upset, Iona accepted Julia's decision. "We could stick with our plan to find a city with electricity. But I'll go with you." She laughed at their surprised faces. "What's wrong? I'm staying with my niece to keep you from ordering her around," she said to Maxine. Seeing Iona was joking, Maxine laughed. Soon all three of them were laughing and talking, the heated discussion forgotten.

The trio sang songs as they walked. "We're off to see the wizard, the wonderful wizard of Oz..."

* * * * *

Night had fallen. It was dark, so dark, and very cold. So cold it felt like the dead of winter. He felt nothing. His piercing eyes focused on the little boy and his mother walking hand in hand. They were oblivious to his stares. He could hear faint strains of a melody above the whistling of the wind. It was the woman singing to her son.

He ignored the twinge of something deep in his being. He leaped out of the bush and onto his shocked prey.

The woman screamed as Ahriman clawed her again and again. Over and over he slashed her skin until she could only whimper. Then, there was silence.

A sudden long, mournful wail broke the silence. The little boy stared at the bloody remains of his mother. He stared but for a moment before, in one decapitating blow, Ahriman ended the boy's life.

A slight gasp from a corner of the dark went unnoticed. Hidden in the shadows appeared a lone figure, bundled up from head to toe. It was he who made the noise. He stole away quickly, silently, into the night.

Ahriman finished his meal and wandered away in the opposite direction from his observer.

Climbing over and around the crap piled in the street, the mysterious stranger paused, out of breath, in a narrow alley. He looked apprehensively behind him to see if he had been followed and relief flared to see that he had not. He was safe, for the moment.

Guilt-ridden, knowing he held responsibility for this new horror facing the world, he fell into a troubled sleep. Tossing and turning on a pile of rags, he cried out in the darkness. His nightmare became more vivid. . .

. . .in a lab, alone except for his equipment and animals. He activates a program on his computer. Lights flash.

An unnerving screech jolts him.

He spins around in his swivel chair.

In the cage sleeps the result of a terrible unpredicted consequence of his experiments.

His portable television flickers. He moves his eyes to the screen, distracted by what he sees. A sign appears. People babble excitedly. Biological warfare. Death. He looks back at his mutation.

At least it will die, he thinks. Then his world goes black…

The man woke from the dream memory drenched in a cold sweat. Night closed in around him, seeming angry, as if knowing the part he played in the devastation. He struggled to push back the night, glancing wildly around him, while his beating heart slowed to an almost normal rate. With his head in his hands, the man sighed.

"All my fault, he should have died! No, I should have killed him. Why didn't you die?" he demanded, raising his fists to the blackened sky. In anguish, he slumped to the ground and willed himself to sleep more.

Rambling around in the dark, gurgling, digesting his recently completed meal, Ahriman remembered a time when he existed as just a nearly insentient laboratory animal. It was a long time ago, but he knew no sense of time. Like a drunken man, he swayed from side to side struggling to maintain balance. Pictures flitted across his rapidly receding gray matter. He vaguely recalled the last thing he saw before the change. It was a male human in a white coat. Ahriman could not remember the male's name.

All of the memories tired Ahriman. Confusion reigned as visions of hypodermic needles, sponges, medicines, and the male passed fleetingly through his muddled mind. He grunted and yawned before descending into a dream. . .

. . .darkness, flashing lights, high-pitched yells; hunger settled on the newly created beast like a blanket from a baby's crib.

Visions of bloodstained clothing, the rotting flesh of humans and animals he had maimed and killed.

A blinding light, representing good in the world. With a single crushing blow, someone extinguished the light. Destroyed good.

But what was this?

A pinpoint of light in the shape of a young human. Another human joined her, and another. The pinpoint increased. Now a fourth shape, a man in a white coat.

The four of them approached him and the closer they got the brighter the light became. The light overpowered him, and good had won. . .

Disgruntled, Ahriman hauled himself up. He shook his head from side to side trying to shake off the nightmare. He knew he must find those four before they uncovered the secret, the reason for being.

A puff of smoke and the entity appeared, hovering above the surprised figure of Ahriman. This entity, the master of illusion, could manifest as anything he wanted to. Many called him a demon. He controlled visions and could create illusions that confused and coerced mortals. These realistic illusions usually could be described as figments of the recipient's imagination. Sometimes, however, they were real.

Disoriented by the puff of smoke, Ahriman looked around, bewildered.

"Up here, ugly. It's your true maker. Aren't you going to say hello?" the little demon chortled, his appearance as a leprechaun oddly fitting. Although Ahriman had never seen the leprechaun before, he recognized the voice and growled. The leprechaun laughed.

"Now, now, mutt. Is that any way to treat me, the mighty one? By the way, the name's MacGregor."

Ahriman, standing now, reached up to swat MacGregor with a giant claw. MacGregor floated out of reach.

"What's wrong with you? You can't hurt me," MacGregor told him, serious for a moment. "I've explained that to you." He rolled his eyes. Dealing with those beneath him could be so tiring.

* * * * *

Ahriman wasn't the only one not getting any sleep that lonely night. Guilt, manifesting itself in a recurring nightmare, prevented the mysterious stranger from sleeping for more than two or three hours at a time. He longed for the brightness and security of the day.

The man staggered to his feet. He yelled out into the oppressive night. "Back, back, all of you evil demons!" Surprised at the volume of his voice and the echoes bouncing all around him, the man stood silently for a long time.

"Excuse me, but can I be of assistance?" The quiet voice brought him back to an awareness of his surroundings. His harsh intake of breath when he saw his visitor punctuated the night. "I am Sister Marie. You seem to be in distress."

"Sister, I am not a Catholic and you are not a priest, but will you hear my confession? I think I may go crazy if I don't tell someone." The man stared at the nun.

"I will listen to your story," Sister Marie assured the man before her.

"I am Dr. Anthony Drew and I made a big mistake." Trembling, the doctor sat on the ground. "I didn't want to create this thing, not this monster. He was supposed to be good, not this evil, foul thing. I created this animal, but someone else corrupted him. It wasn't me. It. Is. Not. My. Fault!" Anthony yelled at the top of his lungs, hoping to assuage himself of the guilt he harbored. "I, a man sworn to save lives, am the sole creator of the evil Ahriman."

He hung his head in shame, but the nun did not reprimand him. She placed her hand gently on his shoulder.

"How did all of this happen? It doesn't sound like you were the only one involved," she observed.

"I was a geneticist and I played God. I admit it. I created, over a thirty-year time span, a lethal hybrid of man, ape, and technology. I implanted a biochip in my ape-man to control him. You see," the doctor hesitated, "Ahriman had the capacity to kill and the yearning to do so. To prevent that if he ever escaped, I assured he would have no cognitive thought unless I told it to him."

"How was a creature created with no thought, but the ability and desire to commit murder, a good creature?" Sister Marie asked.

"He was going to be a programmable watchdog for the public. His sole purpose was to be for defense, but he had an instinct to want to hurt people. The viruses released during the war caused a mutated antibody to speed up his processes, elevated all of his systems. His deadly desires and hunger became almost insatiable. I could see that immediately. Within a few minutes after the initial contamination, I knew he would not get any better, only worse. More and more violent. Yet, I could not kill him," Anthony said this last almost timidly.

"What happened next?" Sister Marie encouraged him.

"Later that day I blacked out while sitting at my computer. When I awoke, Ahriman was gone. I didn't know what had happened or where he had gone. Then, I heard a story about a horrible creature brutalizing a whole family near my lab. I suspected Ahriman, but I couldn't be sure." Anthony frowned at the memory.

"Why couldn't you be sure? Did you think the stories were exaggerations of some other events?"

"No, I just couldn't understand how he had become so aware of himself. In the stories, he is more than sentient, he is… aware," Anthony repeated himself. "The last time I saw him, although stronger and more violent, he did not have conscious thought. I have no idea if the computer chip was functioning at all at that point. He ignored my commands and I couldn't get close enough to him to tranquilize him and check the chip itself. It's all inexplicable," he said in frustration.

"Anthony, what you did was wrong. It seems, however, that whoever knocked you out gave Ahriman his conscious thought and abilities."

"How is that possible?"

"I do not know. I only know that it isn't God's will for a man-beast to roam the country killing people. You must do what you can to stop him."

"You are absolutely right, Sister." Anthony stared into her eyes, and Sister Marie knew they were the eyes of a man on the edge. "I'm sorry. I can't let you tell this story to anyone." Sister Marie didn't struggle, only moved her lips in silent prayer, as Dr. Anthony Drew choked the life out of her.

"I am the resurrection and the life… um, something, something. Go with God, Sister," Anthony finished the funerary services for the nun he had just murdered.

Anthony had no intention of killing Ahriman to right his soul with God. Now that he had told his story he felt immense relief. The relief evaporated when he realized that Ahriman might not have the same benevolent feelings for him. "I'll go to him and tell him I'm sorry. All will be forgiven," Anthony convinced himself. But, if Ahriman would not listen, Anthony would correct his mistake. *To the death,* he thought as he fondled the pickax in his bag.

* * * * *

The new day found Julia, Maxine, and Iona walking approximately in the direction of the North Star, which they could still see shining in the sky. They surmised that maybe it was not the North Star after all. Maxine's dream the night before told her to find the Scepter of Truth. This scepter would protect the people and the scepter was to the north. They would have liked more information to start their journey, but that was all the dream had provided.

So, they decided to go north and find this magic scepter. Iona remained unconvinced that Maxine was the fated heroine. She couldn't quite believe a snotty and ill-prepared child would save the world.

"Iona, what are you thinking about?" Julia asked, noting the sick expression on her aunt's face. "Do you feel okay?"

Iona came out of her reverie and rested her gaze for a moment on her niece before focusing on Maxine. "I was just thinking that she couldn't possibly save the world. She's never even held a real job, I'll bet."

Julia sighed, resigning herself to referee the ensuing fight.

Maxine glared at Iona. "I'm an adult. Of course, I've held a job." She thought for a moment. "I managed one of my father's stores last summer."

"You call that a job!" Iona belly laughed. "Your father gave you that job, you probably weren't paid, and you only had it for a summer." Tears coursed down Iona's cheeks as she tried to control her wild laughter.

Maxine jutted her chin and sat down, pointedly ignoring Iona's chuckles. Julia fumed at both of them.

"What is wrong with you two? First off, Iona, stop baiting Maxine and egging her on. And you," she turned to Maxine, "have to stop taking my aunt seriously." She looked back and forth between them. "We were having such a good time when we put our differences behind us. What made us different is in the past. Let's leave it there and move into the present. Then we can look to the future." She glared at them.

Maxine looked at Iona for her reaction. Iona sighed. "Trite speech, dear. But nonetheless correct. I'm sorry, Maxine. Julia's right. Let's put our differences behind us." She held out her hand. Maxine nodded and shook hands with Iona.

"That was some speech," Maxine told a slightly embarrassed Julia.

"I'm hungry. Do you think we can eat now?" Julia asked, changing the subject.

Iona thought about it and decided the next town should be along before they ran out of their current supplies and starved. She searched through one of the backpacks, considering what food they would eat.

While Iona contemplated their meal, Julia motioned to Maxine to walk over. "Are you sure you can handle anything we might face in tracking and fighting Ahriman?"

Maxine took offense before realizing Julia asked out of concern, not insult. "Absolutely," Maxine answered without a trace of the fear she held in her heart about possibly dying to save the world. Julia smiled in relief and started to turn away. "Wait. I have a question for you."

"What?" Julia asked.

"What happened to your parents?"

Julia thought for a moment, unsure of herself. "My parents gave me to Aunt Iona when I was three years old. They'd been hit with hard times and wanted to get back on their feet before having the responsibility of a toddler. That never happened. Someone murdered my father on his way home from work one day and my mother couldn't take the pain. She killed herself a week after his funeral. Aunt Iona has raised me ever since," she finished solemnly.

"What were your hobbies before the war?" Maxine asked Julia jovially, who smiled weakly at this obvious attempt to lighten the mood. She was about to answer when Iona bustled over to them.

"You two are the first patrons at Iona's Great Restaurant. May I take your order?" Iona asked in a sugary, southern twang. Maxine and Julia laughed and played along.

"I would like crepes suzette and a glass of creme de menthe, Madame," Maxine answered in a perfect French accent. Julia smothered her laughter as Iona and Maxine kept straight faces.

Iona wrinkled her nose. "You want decrepit shoes and cream of moth?" she asked with a thick Brooklyn accent. Julia burst out laughing, wrecking the game.

Maxine and Iona joined in the laughter. Iona winked at Julia, who threw her napkin at her aunt, exclaiming, "You knew what she meant!" Iona grinned impishly.

Maxine jumped into the game, throwing a napkin at Julia. Soon the three travelers were laughing hysterically and throwing balled up napkins at each other. A high-pitched tone caught their attention and they turned in unison toward the sound.

Shrouded in a golden mist, floating above the ground, she appeared to be a goddess. She drifted over on the wind.

"Is it our Fairy Godmother?" Maxine asked mostly in jest.

"I am Alethea, the Mistress of Illusion. I come to seek your help and to help you."

Maxine opened her mouth to speak, but the goddess silenced her with a wave of her hand.

"You do not know," the goddess continued, "that my brother is helping that ghastly Ahriman retrieve the Scepter of Truth before you can." The mistress sighed. "I will follow you throughout your difficult journey. I'll leave you for now, but I will give you one piece of advice. This I direct toward you, Maxine." Alethea stared deep into Maxine's eyes. "Remember what Aesop said. 'Self-conceit may lead to self-destruction.'" She smiled, mouthed goodbye, and vanished.

"What did she mean by that?" Maxine asked. Julia said nothing, but Iona couldn't help her mouth.

"She meant that if you act like a spoiled brat with an oversized ego, you'll ruin everything," Iona said.

Maxine turned to Julia. "Is that what Alethea meant? That my ego could ruin everything?" Julia searched for something to say in response but shrugged.

"My ego won't ruin anything," Maxine said, arms crossed over her chest. "Haven't I been doing well so far?" She stared defiantly at them, her challenge unanswered.

I hope you're right, Julia thought. She had her doubts, as did Iona, who, for once, kept her mouth shut.

"Come on, we still have about five hours of sunlight left," Iona declared, after checking her watch and noting the position of the sun. She signaled them to move.

Maxine jumped to her feet, ready to begin and prove herself worthy. Julia, on the other hand, sat as if in a trance.

Iona snapped her fingers in front of Julia's face. The noise startled her and she stared at Iona. "Are we leaving now? I was just thinking about Alethea," she explained while she stood up.

Julia, Iona, and Maxine continued their journey to truth. One day and one night passed without incident. Too soon they met their first obstacle.

* * * * *

A deep, low rumbling filled the air. Ahriman heaved himself to his feet. He set off in search of food to satisfy his hunger. He roamed for miles before he saw his lunch.

The sun sat high in the clouds and Ahriman's hunger pains intensified. His poisonous mouth watered at the thought of the tender, juicy morsels of human flesh he saw before him. Ahriman raced after his meal. Just as he reached them, they disappeared.

Laughter filled the air while Ahriman growled like a primitive caveman. A puff of smoke and a miniature leprechaun appeared. MacGregor.

Ahriman glared at MacGregor, wishing he could speak. He could only grunt and whine his feelings. MacGregor, who telepathically heard his wish, snickered.

"Oh, Ahriman. You're really hungry, aren't you?" he asked. "I have food for you, but," his voice hardened, "you have to work for it." With that, he pulled a giant chicken out of his pocket. He dangled it enticingly over Ahriman's head.

Ahriman whined and begged, thinking only of the chicken in MacGregor's hand. MacGregor pretended to think about it, even though he already knew what he wanted the beast to do.

"First, I have news for you," MacGregor said. "My sister, Alethea, is helping the enemy." He shook his head. "I don't understand. Does she think she can outsmart me?" he asked himself. Comforted by his belief in his superiority, MacGregor continued.

"At some point, you will meet up with the enemy." He directed Ahriman's attention to a bug that just materialized. "When you meet up with them," his eyes narrowed, "whoever is still alive, I want you to smash them." The bug exploded.

Satisfied he had gotten his point across, MacGregor dropped the chicken to Ahriman and left. Ahriman mauled, mutilated, and finally, devoured the dead chicken. Chicken entrails covered him and he finished them off like a bloodthirsty, hellish barbarian.

Nearby, Dr. Anthony Drew prepared his lunch. After sitting down, he pulled an apple out of his bag. It was a doctor's black bag that still held some of his instruments. He chewed slowly, hoping to make the apple last a long time. He heard a slight noise to his far left. It sounded like an animal eating.

He knew it was Ahriman. The possibility of being so close to the monster chilled his blood, causing a major seizure-like panic attack. His breath quickened, his heart rate accelerated, and he felt as though he would die as he gasped for air. In time this faded and he picked up his apple from the ground, dusted it off, and finished it, ignoring the inhuman gurgles coming from his left. He refused to acknowledge that his connection with Ahriman created a pull that did not allow the two to be far apart, creating his own private Hell on Earth.

Ahriman picked every morsel off the chicken bones. When finished, he licked the blood off his claws. His thoroughness had taken a long time and when he had finished, the sun had dipped farther down the sky. He could pounce and prowl without anyone seeing his grotesque figure, his face reminiscent of a gargoyle's distorted image. The savageness of his meal tired him out, though, so he settled in for a nap.

Drifting off to sleep, he recalled MacGregor's command. He visualized the enemy, a faceless enemy, in place of the bug. He smiled in the dark, as much as he could, at the thought of destroying them. Pleased, he fell asleep with visions of bloody people consuming his thoughts.

* * * * *

Off in a castle on a glistening cliff lived the Entities. Although they disagreed with each other on a lot of things, they followed specific rules and so Alethea could only try to thwart MacGregor, and not stop him herself outright. Soon, she hoped, she would have that ability. When MacGregor arrived home, Alethea immediately challenged him.

"What have you been up to, my evil little brother?" she asked him sweetly.

"I'm so glad you care," he mocked her. "I haven't been up to anything." Alethea stopped him before he left the room.

"Let me tell you something," she said tightly. "I will never allow you to win control of the scepter. I know that's what you're up to," she accused him. MacGregor smiled and waved, then flew off out of her sight. His sister stood behind, not bothering to conceal her anger.

* * * *

The sun had risen over the horizon. It splashed waves of golden warmth down onto the backs of Iona, Julia, and Maxine, waking them from their slumber.

"What an absolutely gorgeous day!" Julia exclaimed.

"It is beautiful," Iona agreed.

Still half asleep, Maxine just nodded. Julia walked around munching on her breakfast, a simple piece of fruit and some bread they had found that wasn't yet stale.

The three heard a loud cheer and a scraggly old man ran toward them. He stopped, out of breath, in front of Maxine. After taking several breaths, he addressed her.

"We knew you would come. Our seer saw you in a dream. Miss, we desperately need your help. The people in my town that survived the war are in dire need of help. Something or someone is kidnapping the people and taking them away, never to be seen again. Please, you must help us." Now the man's eyes widened with fear and he was short of breath again.

Maxine glanced at Iona and Julia before responding. "I feel for you and your town," she began, "but what can I do to help? And how did you see me in a dream?"

Continually glancing behind him, the man spoke to Maxine. "You must find out who is responsible for this and stop them. You are the chosen one. I will take you to my town."

Uncertain, Maxine thought for a moment. "I'll do whatever I can to help."

"Thank you." The man smiled in relief. "I'll show you where to go, just follow." He headed back the direction he came from. Maxine followed behind, with Iona and Julia bringing up the rear. They walked silently.

After walking for an hour, they came upon a street of well cared for homes. The old man stared at the houses.

"I am Mayor Thomson, and this is my town," he told them proudly. "After the last people died, we moved to this block with the few newcomers who came in. Even though it's only been ten days since the war, we already have ten homes on each side and a total of about fifty people living here. We got the electricity on the day after it went out and we all started gardens to harvest when the grocery store food rots away in a few weeks. The disappearances began yesterday, three so far, and we know they will not stop without your help."

Maxine spoke during Mayor Thomson's pause for breath. "Do you have any idea what's happened? Did anybody see or hear anything out of the ordinary?"

"No, it's all been so sudden."

"Who is your seer?" Julia asked.

"She isn't actually a seer," the mayor admitted. "I thought that sounded more interesting." He shrugged. "But, this morning she heard a voice in her head telling her that a trio of women would be traveling right where I found you. The only way for the disappearances to stop was to bring you here to stop them."

"As Maxine said, we'll certainly do all that we can to help you. Do you have any idea what that may be?" Julia asked with uncertainty. The mayor only shrugged again.

Mayor Thomson led Maxine, Iona, and Julia through to the final home on the block. "This is my house. You may stay with me while you're here, if you like," he offered.

"Thank you for your hospitality. We appreciate your invitation," Maxine accepted graciously. Good manners she understood. Behind her, Iona and Julia murmured their thanks.

Looking at his watch, Mayor Thomson determined that dinner would be ready soon.

"I guess we might as well eat now. It'll give us some time to figure out our plan to rid this town of their kidnapper," Iona suggested to her companions. They agreed, their mouths salivating in anticipation of food.

"C'mon down to Town Square. That's the middle of the street where we all eat together for dinner. You can see over there all the stuff being set up." Everyone looked up the block, and indeed it was being prepared for something. "Every afternoon we bring out the material for that night's meal, including food, plates, and utensils. Eating dinner together helps keep us feeling secure and like we're a part of a family," he explained.

Amid much clatter and confusion, Mayor Thomson squeezed the trio into the bustling group of people. Everyone had already heard that these were the women who would protect them. "Each family contributes a part of the meal for the others," he told them, pointing out the salads and several meat dishes. "After a time, we may tire of all the effort for such a large group, preparing varied meals and such. For now, though, everything is still so new. And quiet," he added with a sense of wonder.

The sky overhead darkened; in minutes it appeared the heavens above would open up and pour down on the defenseless Earth. Cries of horror and surprise were heard as the sound of flapping wings became nearly deafening. From out of the sky swooped hundreds of mutated bats. They swarmed over the crowd of people, squealing in hunger.

"It's like something out of *The Wizard of Oz!*" screamed Maxine, as townspeople ran blindly, trying to find their way to their homes.

Mayor Thomson yelled for people to head for cover as best they could. The bats were not allowing anyone to leave Town Square. They kept flying lower and lower, closer to the frightened masses huddling under tables. Julia and Iona ran to where they saw Maxine crouched alone.

"This must be what we were brought here to stop. Does anybody have any suggestions?" Julia questioned, glancing furtively around them and at the sky. Iona shrugged, but Maxine smiled.

"I have an idea, I saw it in a movie once," she announced. "Don't know if it'll work, but it seems we have no choice. I need both of you to help."

"Sure. What do you need us to do?" Julia responded.

"First, we need to get all the matches that people have in their homes. We should be able to slip past these hideous monsters. I've seen a few people make it out." She detailed the rest of her plan. They scattered to gather their supplies.

Soon they returned with matches and makeshift torches. Maxine instructed Iona to pass them out and sent Julia back to the homes for more matches and flammable items.

"Listen. Please calm down and listen," Iona yelled at the frantic crowd, trying to make herself heard. After several attempts, she got the groups closer together and quiet enough for her to be audible over the shrieking bats that continued to dive-bomb them. She gave the outer rim of people large torches. The townspeople used them to smash the bats when they approached. This sent the bats screaming off into the night. The effect was only temporary and soon they came back, one after the other.

Julia, meanwhile, finished her search. She enlisted the help of some men on the fringe edge of the group. They carried several of the larger pieces of wood furniture, insuring that she would possess lots of firewood.

"Maxine, I got everything," Julia yelled. Maxine motioned her over to where she crouched.

"Wonderful. Get those men to help you spread this stuff in a big circle all around the townspeople. Then light it like we discussed. Make sure those torches stay lit," Maxine turned to instruct Iona, who gave her a withering glance. Julia left to spread the wood while Maxine brought into the circle the goods she had gone for earlier.

The town remained gripped in fear, but there was now also a sense of family and team spirit as the town rallied together with torches and a ring of fire. Some of the bats dove past the ring of fire toward the townspeople, who time and again repelled them with torches. A cacophony filled the night. Screams of terror from the townspeople became cheers with each success and soon the bats flew off.

The sound of the final mutated bat died away, replaced by the townspeople's delighted laughter. They doused the torches and fire that had saved their lives with the water bottles and fire extinguishers Maxine had diligently searched for throughout their homes. As the water extinguished the last dying embers, a figure appeared above the three heroines.

"You have done well," the figure spoke to them. "I'm sorry I am unable to help you in situations like this. The three of you battled bravely, the disappearances here will stop, and you are one step closer to finding what you seek."

"Why can't you help us?" Maxine asked in a petulant tone, belying the strong woman deeply hidden underneath that had briefly emerged to save the town.

"It's useless to explain. I cannot interfere in certain things in your realm."

"What are we searching for?" Julia asked, fearing she already knew the answer.

"Are we searching for that scepter?" Iona questioned Alethea, who held up her hand.

"Please, be quiet. Now is not the time for a discussion," she stated. "You must continue onward. Good luck." She vanished.

Iona pointed behind them. "Look at the sunrise. I can't believe we fought all night," she said in surprise.

"I don't believe it either," Julia agreed. "It seemed to happen so fast."

"It doesn't really matter," Maxine pointed out the obvious. "We need to leave here as soon as we get some rest."

"Do you have to go?" The trio spun around to find Mayor Thomson standing behind them. "Must you go?

You can stay as long as you like. We are forever in your debt," he said.

"We appreciate the thought, but we must continue on," Maxine explained. Mayor Thomson shook their hands and thanked them profusely.

"There's no need. We did what was right," Maxine contended. Julia and Iona echoed her sentiments. "I'm sure you'll have no more trouble with those bats or with the disappearances," she assured the mayor.

"I sincerely hope you're right," the mayor said, as he led them to his home so they could rest and prepare for their journey.

* * * * *

"I can't believe it!" a voice shouted. "I refuse to believe it!"

"Believe it, little brother. It's true," Alethea smugly informed her brother.

"I can't believe it," MacGregor repeated. "Those bats should have finished them."

"Sorry to disappoint you," she said. "You underestimated the power of those three. I expect the disappearances of those townspeople will stop."

"They'll stop," he grumbled.

"Take this defeat to heart. You will fail," Alethea promised him.

"We'll see about that," he muttered to himself.

* * * * *

Stumbling across the ground, Dr. Anthony Drew saw people. Rubbing his eyes, he wondered if it was another mirage. He half ran, half stumbled over to the group. They were cleaning up burnt wood, talking and laughing.

"Somebody help me," he cried out weakly. "I ran out of food days ago and when I found food in a house, I think it poisoned me. Please help me."

A young woman approached. "Hello," she greeted the doctor. "I'm Melissa. Welcome."

"Please," Anthony begged again, "may I have something to ease the pain? My stomach is killing me." The stranger appeared ill and dehydrated.

Melissa led him to the doctor's house. "What do we have here?" the jovial man asked as the two entered his home.

"Probable food poisoning," Melissa answered for Anthony, who just groaned.

"Don't worry, fella. We'll fix you right up. Where you headed anyway?" Anthony didn't answer and seemed to not appreciate the doctor's attempts at conversation. The doctor finished the examination in silence, concluding that the poisoning had almost run its course.

"We'll give you a little something to help it along and ease the pain. You have to stay here for a day or so," the doctor told him.

"Fine, fine. When do you think I'll be able to hold something down? Despite the pain, I'm starving," Anthony said.

"That's a good sign. You could probably have some light broth. I'll have Melissa fetch you some. Do you mind?" He directed this last at Melissa, who assured him it was no problem.

Fifteen minutes later, Melissa returned with a pot of soup and a bowl. She gave some to Anthony, who carefully and slowly ate it.

"What's going on with the cleanup? Did you have a fire?" Anthony asked.

"Yes, we had a huge bonfire in the middle of the street. To ward off the giant bats," she explained. That got his attention and she told him the whole story. When she finished, the bell ringing in his head would not be quiet. And then he realized why.

"Three women traveling alone were foreseen to help you with your problem?"

"Oh yes!" she answered, going on and on about what the three looked like and how they acted.

Anthony wasn't fully listening. He sensed that these three were important to him.

"Did they say where they were going?" He startled Melissa, and himself, with his question.

"What, huh, no. No, they didn't," Melissa replied. "Why do you want to know? Do you know them?" She asked this in a guarded tone, despite her attempt to keep it light.

Anthony hedged around the question, laughing to relieve the sudden tension. "I believe I might have met them. You must admit, three women alone stick out," he offered as an explanation.

Looking him over once more, Melissa accepted the explanation and relaxed. "Sure, they would."

Days later, with a full stomach, a clear head, and a bag full of food, Dr. Anthony Drew headed off in the direction of the trio. He remembered his dream before coming into the town and what it had said... and realized the importance of the three women.

. . .*the swirling light spun around, growing in intensity until it reached a monstrous size and burst, showering light onto the land. He found himself among a group of strangers who appeared unaware of his presence. He moved between them, intrigued by his invisibility. The group had an older woman, two girls, a beautiful translucent woman, a leprechaun, and. . . Ahriman! He stared in fascinated shock at the evil creature he created. He heard a voice in the air.*

Dr. Anthony Drew, welcome to the happy world of your innermost thoughts and feelings, *the voice began.*

Who are you? *he inquired, anxiously looking for the source of the voice.*

You cannot see me, *the voice chuckled dryly.* That is unimportant. The group before you may appear carefree, but they have troubled souls, not unlike your own, doctor. The older woman, the girls, and the shimmering woman are Good. With a capital G. *The voice paused.* The leprechaun and the creature are Evil. With a capital E. They are all on a quest, for very different reasons, in search of the Scepter of Truth. The scepter makes the world an understandable place to live. The scepter enables living beings to distinguish illusion from reality. In the wrong hands, no one would know what was real and chaos would run rampant over the land. Watch and remember, Doctor.

The voice stopped and the vision changed. High upon a mountain, surrounded by a valley of unimaginable depths, Anthony found himself an unseen spectator in a showdown between the members of the group he had previously observed. They faced one another, knowing the fight would end only with the death of the opposition.

Wait, *he called out.* Not everyone is there. Where are—

The voice interrupted. Do not ask questions. The hour grows late and I cannot tell you more. Remember what you have seen. *The voice quieted. . .*

Dr. Anthony Drew did not understand what he was supposed to understand from his dream. Who was the voice and who were the people? These unidentified people were going to duke it out. For what? The fate of the world? Even now, after hearing about the girl from the mayor, he could not decipher the hidden message in his somewhat obscure dream.

* * * * *

Ahriman was hungry. For some unknown reason, he could not find any food. The air swirled and Ahriman waited expectantly, knowing what was coming. MacGregor appeared, with a wide grin on his face and a bloody chicken in his hand. Ahriman drooled as he watched the chicken swinging back and forth like a pendulum.

MacGregor laughed his horrible laugh, like fingernails on a chalkboard, and called to Ahriman. "Are you hungry?" he asked, the answer obvious. "Listen to me carefully." Ahriman listened, his eyes never leaving the carcass.

"Travel in the direction you have been traveling in, but go faster. Rest only when you absolutely have to, and only for a few hours. It is imperative you catch up with the trio I spoke of before. Never hesitate. Push onward, always, at any cost. You must find them and destroy them!" MacGregor screamed his orders. Dropping the chicken, he vanished.

Ahriman leaped hungrily onto the chicken, at once savoring it and tearing it to pieces with his claws. He didn't stop his attack until he finished his entire meal, bones and all. Licking his bloodstained claws, he continued his pursuit of the humans.

* * * * *

...Maxine ran faster and faster, unable to escape the enemy closing in on her. She tripped over a large root and hit her head

when she landed. Her last thought as the darkness enveloped her was to save the others.

A cool hand rubbed her face. No, water dripped on her. Opening her eyes, Maxine found that it was drizzling. She stood, amazed to be alive.

A dot of light in the distance approached, growing stronger. Maxine saw that it appeared to be an angel. Maybe I'm dead, she thought. Did it rain in heaven?

Maxine smiled when she saw who the angel was. Alethea, *she tried to say, but no sound emerged. Words formed in her mind from Alethea.*

Maxine, *Alethea began.* You must travel faster. My brother has sent a demon to destroy you and your friends. The scepter grows dimmer with each passing moment. You must reach it soon; we must not allow the scepter to fade into non-existence. If you do not reach the Scepter of Truth, all will be lost. You must beat them at their own game.

Don't speak in riddles! *Maxine cried out silently.* Who are they? Who is in league with your brother against us? *Alethea shook her head and smiled.*

Go on, my young heroine. I will help you when I can, but I cannot interfere with destiny. *Alethea waved goodbye and faded from view. As Alethea dissipated, the darkness returned.*

Maxine heard voices and the darkness retreated. She awoke and looked into the face of a concerned Julia.

"Maxine, wake up. You were talking in your sleep," Julia said.

Maxine looked around in confusion. Then she understood. It had been a dream. "Julia," she shouted, grabbing her shoulders. "Alethea came to me in a dream. She said evil is edging closer, and every day brings us nearer to the scepter." Excitement animated Maxine's face as she recounted the dream to Julia and Iona.

Maxine spoke of the unknown terror stalking them. She told them the consequences of their failure.

"We will not fail," declared Julia. Iona cheered in agreement, but Maxine smiled uneasily.

"We will not fail," Maxine agreed, without conviction. She changed the subject to safety. "We must find weapons to defend ourselves against the evil coming."

Julia agreed, but Iona had a question. "If we don't know what's after us, how will we know what to use to defend ourselves?" she asked. Maxine frowned.

"Anything will help. I didn't get the impression that those after us were anything supernatural. Besides, just having any weapons should boost our morale," Maxine responded. Iona agreed with her and the three went about the arduous task of assembling weapons.

Each of them went in different directions with the same intent – if you see anything that might be useful, grab it. They scrounged around, rummaging through empty houses, peering into every nook and cranny for about four hours. They returned to the meeting place to compare their findings.

"What did we find?" Maxine asked. For the next hour, they pored over their findings, keeping the most useful and tossing the rest aside. When they finished, they stood back to take a look.

Maxine whistled in appreciation. "This is amazing," she said in wonder.

The women had gathered hunting knives, kitchen knives, complete bows and arrows, and even found one working pistol, fully loaded. They divided up the arsenal, with Maxine holding the gun. She argued successfully that she was the only one trained to fire a gun. They headed north until it was too dark to see. After stashing everything out of sight, they settled in for the night.

The next morning, Maxine, Iona, and Julia had been traveling for about two hours past sunrise when the first signs of trouble appeared. They had come across several old campfires and, in the distance, saw a group huddled together. Iona whispered for her companions to be quiet and they attempted to pass around the group unnoticed.

With a warlike howl, the huddled group disbanded, scattering in all directions. The land took on a deathly silence. The three women advanced, senses heightened, watching for signs of attack. They searched so hard for minuscule signs that a full-scale attack took them by surprise. The attackers looked like the vagrants and scum of the old world. A band of seven descended on the women. Brandishing weapons, the trio fought back.

Maxine shot and killed two of the attackers, a middle-aged man and a younger woman. Julia stabbed another in the gut when he attempted to snatch her knapsack of supplies. Iona got two men of her own before a third stabbed her from behind through her lower back. Maxine took out the final two with the pistol and the fight was over. Seven dead, one wounded.

"Aunt Iona, how bad does it feel?" Iona didn't answer, but appeared to be in shock. Julia struggled not to cry.

"Listen," Maxine began, "we need to keep her calm. Your crying will upset her."

"Upset her! She isn't even aware of what's going on," Julia hollered.

Ignoring Julia's anger, Maxine turned her attention to Iona, who was regaining awareness.

Unaware that anyone observed their actions, Maxine and Julia looked at Iona's wound. They couldn't tell if any major damage had occurred. Searching through the first aid kit, they found antiseptic, bandages, and a mild painkiller. Julia cleaned the wound and applied the bandages. After Iona took the medicine, she drifted off to sleep, with Julia and Maxine keeping a concerned vigil.

MacGregor had glared in anger as he had watched his recruits get massacred by the three mortal women. Now, noting the older woman's wound, he vanished.

* * * * *

Ahriman lifted his head, all of his senses alert. Off to the right, something moved, drawing his attention. He snarled a warning in the direction of the movement. A man stepped out from behind a mountain of garbage, ignoring the warning.

"Ahriman," the man said hesitantly. Ahriman narrowed his eyes at the use of his name. The two slowly approached each other. Ahriman's blood froze when he recognized the identity of the strange man before him.

Visions of cages and needles filled his mind, and he advanced with a growl. The man, too, came forward, but unafraid. The lack of fear startled Ahriman; he had never seen it before.

"Ahriman," the man said again. "Remember me? It's Anthony Drew." He glanced around, taking in the surrounding area. "We," he whispered, "will join as equals and search for the scepter."

The beast startled at the word scepter. He stared at Anthony, trying to determine where the man might have heard about the scepter. The only conceivable place, he thought, was with the women.

As if reading his thoughts, Anthony shook his head, laughing. "No, I haven't been talking with them." He said this last with a snort of contempt. The mad eyes blazed. "I saw it in a dream," he spoke wonderingly. "Everyone was in it. You, those angel things, the women." Ahriman's suspicions abated; he doubted even the creepy doctor would say he saw it in a dream unless he did.

"So, you see," Anthony continued. "We must work together if we are to successfully defeat them and find the scepter first." Ahriman looked at the doctor, respect dawning in his eyes. Anthony saw it and knew now was the time to cement the deal. He walked up to the beast and offered his hand. Shocked, Ahriman accepted the gesture with only a moment's hesitation. Creator and creation were reunited. A deadly team reborn.

MacGregor observed Ahriman sleeping beside Anthony. "Ahriman," he whispered. "Ahriman, come over here." The beast lifted his head at the sound of his name. Seeing MacGregor off to the side, he approached. "I want to talk about your union with the good doctor," the leprechaun said.

Ahriman snarled and MacGregor laughed. "I want you to stay with Doctor Drew for now," MacGregor informed him. "But, if I say to end it, you will. And with no discussion." Ahriman nodded. "Just know that the situation is temporary. And watch your back, the doc's not dealing in reality."

* * * * *

Julia awoke to the sound of her aunt crying in her sleep. She woke Maxine, and they hurried to Iona's side. Julia kneeled next to the moaning woman. "Aunt Iona, wake up," she whispered. Iona slowly opened her eyes. Seeing the worried looks in their faces, she offered them a weak smile. She opened her mouth to speak.

"Iona, don't say anything and don't move," Maxine urged her. She gestured for Julia to follow her and they walked several feet away. "Why did you wake her up?"

Julia continued to watch her aunt while responding. "Because she was crying."

"Did she say anything?"

Julia shook her head and tears brimmed.

Maxine rushed to speak. "It's a good thing you're up. It's time to move on. Whoever is racing us draws nearer and we must hurry. There's a cave to the northeast. To enter the cave, we must cross a deep ravine. Just getting to the ravine would be difficult enough for Iona, but it would be impossible to cross. I think it would be best to make her as comfortable as possible here and continue on without her." Maxine stopped and watched Julia for a reaction.

"Before we discuss Aunt Iona, I'd like to know where you got this information and why we want to enter this particular cave."

"I dreamed about the cave with the scepter. Iona was not in it," Maxine said simply. Now Julia gaped at her.

"You saw it in a dream?" she questioned. Maxine nodded in irritation. With a flash of clarity, Julia understood. Alethea must have told Maxine in a dream. Julia grinned sheepishly. "I guess that's that. What do you think we should do?" she asked Maxine, indicating Iona.

The two walked back over to where the older woman sat dozing. "Iona," Julia said. Her aunt's eyes snapped open.

"Before either of you say anything," Iona started, "I have something to say first. I don't know what the two of you were talking about, but I suspect it concerns me." She held up a hand to silence their immediate protests. "Don't deny the truth. It's okay." She smiled kindly. "You must go on without me. I will not be talked out of my decision. You will leave me here with food, a weapon, and some medicine." To her surprise, neither of them protested. In fact, she thought she noticed Julia sigh in relief.

Julia hugged her aunt fiercely. "You're very brave." She steadied her trembling voice. "Maxine and I will find a safe place for you to wait for our return with the scepter." Iona agreed and fell asleep while Julia and Maxine hastened their search for a shelter. They felt time slipping away.

By mid-afternoon, Maxine had fashioned a shelter for Iona, while Julia set up rocks and debris to hide her aunt from view, should any travelers pass that way. The three women agreed that Iona would be better off here in the relative open, rather than attempt to move her to some remote location. Satisfied with their work, Julia and Maxine helped Iona into her home for the next few days. Julia prayed they were not longer than a week. Iona already looked worse. She had lost a lot of blood and the risk of infection remained ever present.

Julia and Maxine set off at once, although only a few hours of daylight remained. They covered ground faster without Iona to hinder their progress. It had been dark for many hours when they made camp for the night. Their sleep was scant; and after a restless night, they rose with the sun, continuing on their way.

Around noon, Julia saw what looked to be a falling off in the distance. "It's the ravine," she cried. They pushed on, traveling even quicker than before. They reached the ravine's edge at nightfall. Julia judged passing through the ravine at night to be too dangerous, so they decided to wait for morning. After hours of staring into an unusually empty sky, they finally fell into an uneasy sleep.

The next morning's rising sun promised a bright day. Julia and Maxine packed up camp, each thinking ahead to what could come. They started down the ravine before the sun had been in the sky an hour.

Julia followed Maxine as she inched her way down the side of the ravine. They said nothing during the treacherous descent. Several hours later they reached the bottom. It was about five miles across. They figured they could walk to where they would begin their ascent and then camp for the night.

No words passed between them until about two miles across when Julia fell. Her yelp broke the stillness in the air. Maxine turned around in time to see Julia hit the ground. Maxine rushed to her side.

"Julia, are you okay? What happened?" The other woman didn't look hurt, but she was crying hard. Although, Maxine thought her crying looked suspiciously like laughing. When Maxine realized that Julia really was laughing, she watched for some sign of lunacy. Seeing Maxine's expression doubled Julia's laughter.

"What are you laughing at?" Maxine asked, baffled.

Laughing harder still, Julia sputtered, "Look at what I tripped over." Curious, Maxine peered where Julia pointed. Maxine smirked in understanding. Then she laughed. Julia had tripped over a sign that read *Watch your step, loose rocks*. Under that message, some wit had added *and other assorted items like signs*. The added portion appeared recent.

"I don't believe it. Who would have added that?" Maxine questioned her. "We're in the middle of miles of uninhabited forest." They stopped laughing, realizing the possible significance of their find.

"Someone was here recently," Julia stated. Maxine agreed that was probably true and helped Julia off of the ground. Unable to determine what significance the sign held, they continued onward, soon forgetting the sign. Neither one peered back, but if they had, they would have seen a peculiar sight. The sign Julia had tripped over moments before vanished into the air as if it had never existed at all.

Julia stared at her watch. "It must have been shorter across than we guessed," she surmised. Maxine gave her a distracted look, absorbed in the work of trying to carve a stick. It helped Maxine think, she discovered, and it passed the time. "We still have plenty of time for the trip up the ravine. But, we shouldn't," Julia concluded, mystified. "We should have to make camp."

Maxine shrugged. "We made a minor miscalculation. Let's use it to our advantage and be out of the ravine by nightfall."

Julia reluctantly agreed, unable to understand the apparent time distortion. She forgot about her suspicions as the duo began the dangerous climb out of the ravine. Several hours later they reached their destination and settled in for the night. As Julia drifted off to sleep, she remembered the time problem and contemplated explanations. She could only find two and one was not plausible. Exhausted, she cleared her mind and followed Maxine in deep slumber.

* * * * *

Iona lifted her head, hearing something. She had been patiently sitting in her hiding place, drifting in and out of consciousness, taking her pain pills. Now, she sat listening to sounds that might be voices.

Yes, voices were approaching where Iona sat hiding. She began to rise, paused, unsure. Deciding that the voices sounded ominous, she lurched to her feet. She saw the travelers just before they saw her and painfully knew that she'd likely give up her life to help her niece and Maxine.

"Hello," Iona called out with feigned cheerfulness. "Where are you headed?" She grimaced in agony as a wave of pain swept through her body. She stared at her new companions, trying to conceal her shock. The man appeared mad as he took her in with his strange eyes. The other one, she shuddered, was obviously not human.

Ahriman and the doctor witnessed Iona's grimace, despite her efforts to hide the pain. Anthony recognized her from his dream, knew she was important somehow, but Ahriman did not. He growled at Iona, earning a look of reproach from the doctor. Anthony smiled disarmingly.

"You must forgive him; he isn't feeling quite himself today," he explained. "He has mutated cell disorder," he creatively diagnosed Ahriman. Pretending to just notice her injury, his face assumed a mask of concern. "I see you're wounded. May I ask what happened, or offer assistance? I'm a doctor." Iona eyed him, knowing not to trust the wide-eyed man and his monster. But she smiled at him anyway, recognizing the need to stall the pair from traveling further.

"I was attacked," Iona said.

"Was anyone else in your party hurt?" Anthony asked.

Iona answered slowly, deliberately, wondering in her head if he knew there were others or if he was fishing for information. "My only traveling partner died some time ago. I've been wandering alone ever since." The man seemed to believe her. He smiled sympathetically.

"I'm sorry that you were attacked." He unexpectedly blushed in embarrassment. "My name is Adam Johnson and he is Jeff Jacobson."

Iona nodded, figuring he was lying. Extending her hand, she replied, "Nice to meet you. My name is Rebecca Nicholson."

He shook her hand. He figured that she had lied. Anthony opened his mouth to speak, but Ahriman's roar drowned out whatever he said – right before the beast attacked Iona.

While Anthony screamed for him to stop, Ahriman strangled a terrified Iona to death. She fought to free herself from Ahriman's vise-like grip, her fingers digging into the meaty flesh of his arms. The life ebbed from her and her arms fell to her sides. After he choked every bit of life from her, Ahriman dropped the lifeless body on the ground. Anthony stared in shock at the woman crumpled on the ground. He turned to face Ahriman.

"What the hell did you do that for?" he screamed at the monster. "You didn't have to kill her, you moron." Ahriman regarded the doctor malevolently and Anthony sensed the unspoken danger.

Anthony's eyes became dull gray marbles floating in his face. He motioned for Ahriman to follow and the pair continued on in silence.

* * * * *

"Oh no," Maxine moaned. The entrance to the cave and the walk in had so far proven uneventful. Here, however, a potential problem loomed in the form of a fork in the cave's path. She looked concerned, but Julia didn't hesitate.

"We'll have to split up," she said.

"I was afraid you would say that," Maxine responded. "You take the right. I'll take the left. I'm sure we'll be fine."

"You've really taken charge during this journey. I didn't think you had it in you," Julia acknowledged.

"I've gained it through watching my elders," Maxine responded with a smile.

"See you soon," Julia promised, her voice cracking. Maxine hugged her before they set off in their separate directions.

* * * * *

Ahriman stopped and, looking around, growled at an unseen enemy.

Anthony stiffened, asking, "What is it?"

Ahriman gestured back the way they came.

The doctor could see the ravine up ahead. He pointed to it. "Look how close we are," he whispered hungrily. "Let's hurry so we can get on with it." Ahriman looked at him, his eyes veiled. Anthony worried when he saw those eyes fixed on him that way and he kept his guard up as he searched for whatever Ahriman had growled at. He kept his guard up too much and it almost cost him his life.

The doctor heard his attacker before he saw him, but misjudged the direction. Pain consumed his body as a sharp object slashed through his shoulder. He turned to see Ahriman's claw just before he felt it slash his chest wide open. He tried to speak through a mouthful of his own blood. Staring at Ahriman in terror, his own death flashed before him.

Noooo, his mind screamed. *This inhuman creature will not kill me.* Anthony pulled the pickax out of his bag and swung at Ahriman. Surprised by the weapon, Ahriman briefly stood motionless. The pause was enough. Barely. The pickax connected with Ahriman's meaty neck, killing him. The doctor gazed down upon the corpse of his own creation. Ignoring his own wounds, Drew staggered on toward the ravine.

The race wasn't over yet.

* * * * *

In the darkness, Julia realized the farther she walked the more she could see clearly. She figured her eyes had adjusted to the dark, but the adjustment seemed too fast. Then she noticed a faint glow from the walls. Julia ran her fingers over the softly glowing rock.

"Amazing," she whispered. Transfixed by the effervescent wall, Julia didn't hear the rumbling until it was too late.

The ceiling appeared to be caving in, but it was not. Julia had set off a booby trap. The rocks came from an unnoticed crevice high on the wall, creating the illusion of a ceiling caving in. Julia didn't think of any of this, however, as the ton of rocks crashed to the floor around her. Screaming, she attempted to outrun her fate, but it was not to be. When the rocks ceased to fall, only silence remained. The fallen rock had buried Julia.

Maxine noticed the glowing walls as Julia did. Unaware of Julia's accident, Maxine nevertheless remained cautious of potential pitfalls. She walked slowly down the center of the cave, not touching anything, glancing around often. Nobody could live with her cautious, perfectionist father for all those years and not have something rub off. She passed into the center of the maze without incident.

The light grew stronger until Maxine could not look straight ahead. Forced to stare at her feet, she hoped not to hit anything. She sensed the object blocking her path before she saw its bottom. An immense luminous object stood before her. Upon seeing its base, Maxine determined the object was a great door, possibly the only thing standing between her and the scepter. She reached out her hand.

Maxine shook as electricity flowed through her body. With great effort, she pulled her hand away. The current stopped when she broke contact with the door, but her body continued to twitch. Incredible pain filled her. She felt herself slipping away, losing the battle with the darkness. Suddenly a voice filled her mind. Alethea spoke to Maxine, but she could not make out the words. She struggled to listen and received a riddle as a reward for her troubles. *Purity of soul will unlock the truth.*

Still stinging with the aftershocks, but no longer in fear of a blackout, her mind considered the riddle. *What could it mean?* Maxine wondered. She struggled to understand the meaning, her mind grasping an idea that might work. Facing the door, she stared into the blinding light.

Maxine cleared her mind of excess thoughts. Her arms dangled by her sides. She focused on a single sentence. *I am pure.* She chanted in her mind.

I am pure.

Certain she would succeed, amazement nevertheless filled her body when the door slid open. Light lessened to the point of mere illumination and Maxine stared at the end of her journey.

* * * * *

Crossing the ravine had taken the better part of the day, but to Anthony, the effort was well worth it. He entered the cave before him quickly, knowing that the game neared its conclusion. He trotted through the dark hallways until he came to the fork Julia and Maxine had passed. Pausing a fraction of a second, he chose the path to the right and quickened his pace.

Anthony barely noticed the illuminated walls that had captivated the women. He fantasized about finding the scepter. So preoccupied was he that he was unaware of the rocks blocking his path until he tripped over one. He contemplated the best way to climb over them. A rustling to his left diverted his attention from the task at hand. He cautiously approached and was stunned to see a girl partially trapped under a section of rock. She looked bruised, but none of her injuries appeared life threatening. She gazed at him beseechingly.

"Please," she whispered. "Help me. I'm stuck." The doctor considered his options. He shrugged and continued on his way, choosing to leave her there.

"Wait! Please," the girl called out to the retreating figure. Anthony ignored her pleading calls and when her cries were no longer audible, relief coursed through him. A man with a mission had no time to aid the enemy. He sped up his walking until he sprinted down the glowing halls, despite his injuries.

Sprawled on the ground, the doctor cursed spiritedly. He had been so oblivious to his surroundings as he charged like a raging bull down the hall that he missed the outstretched foot that tripped him (again). Anthony sprang to his feet and turned to face his unknown assailant.

Out of the shadows came a creature so hideous and deformed it might have been cast out of the well of insanity. Anthony stared at the creature as it moved in for an attack. At the threat to his life, the doctor drew his pickax. His wounds burned while he blindly swung the ax in the creature's general direction. As luck would have it, the strike hit home, taking the creature's arm off. Howling, it sliced through the air with the remaining arm. This, too, hit home, and the retaliating shot removed Anthony's ear.

Pain exploded inside his body, spurring him to action. With a mighty yell, the doctor charged this creature who had the audacity to challenge him in this deadly game. By pure desire to annihilate, Anthony slammed the ax into the creature's chest again and again until both the creature and the doctor fell to the ground. Exhaustion that had been creeping up stole over him as he lay panting.

While the good doctor lay sleeping next to his victim, Julia was wide awake, frantically trying to free herself from the rock prison. Her anger at being left to die fueled her strength, allowing her to move enough of the hated rock to wiggle out. Once free of her imprisonment, Julia flicked the small rocks caught in her short hair and clothes and set off in the direction the man had traveled earlier. She ignored the pain of her multiple abrasions, concentrating on only the scepter.

"I must get to the scepter," she repeated to herself whenever the pain became too great. She hoped to find that lousy man who left her, but that would be just a bonus. Her main objective was to find the scepter. If the man interfered with her quest, she would tear his eyes out and feed them to him. Smiling with grim pleasure at the thought, Julia pressed forward down the hallway toward the man and the scepter.

* * * * *

Maxine entered the room humbly as if entering a chapel. She approached the object suspended in midair. She stared at the scepter, awestruck by what it represented. The answers to life were at her fingertips. She needed only to reach forward and pick it up.

Unknown to Maxine, Alethea was spiritually in the room as well. She and her brother could not physically penetrate this mystical chamber. Although Maxine could neither see nor hear her, Alethea screamed at the young woman to grasp the scepter. Maxine didn't know she had deactivated the electrical blocks on the other doors.

Anyone could get in now, just by pushing the door open.

So taken in by the beauty of the scepter, Maxine lost her advantage. Anthony entered the room from another door and crept up behind her.

Thanks to his catnap, however, Julia hadn't been far behind the doctor. Motivated by the vision of Maxine being hacked to death, she flung herself at Anthony's back and tackled him.

Maxine turned from the scepter at the sound of the commotion in time to see Anthony stab Julia for her valiant efforts. Crying out, she fell off the doctor, clutching her wounded side. He raised his bloodstained ax, intending to finish off the annoying girl. Maxine unsheathed her knife and slid it between Anthony's shoulder blades. Julia screamed as his body toppled over on her. By the time Maxine removed the body, Julia had passed out from the shock. Maxine wearily sat down beside her to rest.

A short while later, a sense of urgency filled Maxine. She extended her hand toward the scepter. Julia awakened in time to witness the scepter float into Maxine's outstretched fingers. It felt cool yet vibrant, full of a calm energy. The surrounding walls crumbled. Julia's pain diminished then vanished altogether. As they watched with complete serenity, the entire maze around them collapsed to the ground.

Wind blew forcibly at their tired bodies while they watched a familiar figure appear. Alethea stood before them, waiting. Maxine handed her, with no ceremony or blaring trumpets, the Scepter of Truth.

"Thank you," Alethea whispered. "Now I can tell you both the importance of the scepter. You may have noticed odd things happening as you neared the caves surrounding the scepter. Things appearing where they shouldn't be, beings coming from nowhere, strange lights or sounds. This is because of the scepter. The Scepter of Truth keeps illusion and reality separate and distinguishable. Without it, life would be for the entire world as the last few days were for you. You would never know if what you were seeing was real. The illusions people would see would reflect aspects of their own psyche. Can you imagine the world this way? You are true heroines for insuring that evil failed to steal the scepter. I must go, but I will return in time."

Maxine and Julia stared after her as Alethea disappeared.

* * * * *

"It's not fair, it's not fair," MacGregor whined.

Alethea smiled contentedly.

He glared at her, eyes watering.

She laughed and began closing the door to the dimension. Pausing, she reminded him, "I told you not to interfere. You did, causing many innocent people to die and endangering the world for your amusement. Now I sentence you to remain outside this dimension as your punishment." She continued to shut the door.

"But three hundred years?" MacGregor yelled after her. Not pausing another second, Alethea closed the doorway firmly. As she activated the psychic lock, a smile of triumph tinged with sadness flitted across her angelic features.

* * * * *

Maxine stared at Julia, eyes wide in amazement. "It's over," she said. "A couple of weeks ago, I had only just left my old life. What an adventure it has been! I found you. We prevented a disaster. Now it's over," she repeated.

Julia shook her head in disagreement. "No," she contradicted. "It's not over. Number one, we have to find my aunt. Number two, we have a brand-new life ahead of us." She beamed. "Let's go find Aunt Iona."

* * * * *

"Oh no, no," Julia cried out, rushing to the figure. Crouching beside the body on the ground, she sobbed.

Maxine stared in astonishment at them both. How could a woman so vibrant and full of life be dead? She bowed her head for the woman before her, remembering all Iona had taught her and how she had given her life for the truth. After a while, the two girls buried the body under a towering tree.

"I am sorry about your aunt and friend," a voice said. Maxine and Julia turned to see Alethea walking toward them. In her hand, she still held the scepter. "I have something of great importance to talk with you about. I have an offer to make the both of you." She watched their faces closely. "I can return the Earth to a state similar to the myth of Eden, where things like war, poverty, and hunger cease to exist."

"Yes, of course, we want that," Maxine enthused.

"We'll do anything. What do you want?" Julia asked.

"The price will be high," Alethea warned, "for this is not a simple gift to provide. You must give up your lives in exchange for the new world."

"I'll do it to give world peace to the survivors," Julia consented.

Maxine looked wary.

"What are you taking so long to decide for?"

"I don't want to die," Maxine confessed quietly.

"Are you kidding? We can save the world."

"Death is a funny concept humans have created," Alethea explained. "All the energy that makes up your body would remain in existence after I remove the shell. You would feel no pain during the release."

"She doesn't care about any of that mystical crap," Julia snapped. "All she cares about is herself. You were right Alethea, her ego will ruin everything."

"Is that what you were talking about when you said that before?" Maxine asked. "How could you know what would happen?"

"I didn't. That statement was a warning based on your past. I am not omniscient," Alethea admitted with a slight smile.

"I think it is ego. I know you like your life as it is, but you could ensure that the world never suffers this way ever again," Julia begged. "And it isn't like the traditional idea of death, anyway."

"Death is death. No matter what fancy philosophy is offered. Incidentally, I have done quite a bit already by saving the world's sanity. We got the Scepter of Truth without dying and I'd rather not give up my life right now."

"You're certainly living up to your spoiled background," Julia spat the words.

"It's not completely ego guiding my decision," Maxine countered. "Think about it. The world becomes Eden, but the people are still the Adams and Eves who got tossed out of the mythical original one. Just because the world is perfect doesn't mean it will remain so. Can you promise us that the world would never revert to prewar conditions?" Alethea shook her head. "Of course you can't. You already said you couldn't tell the future – except based on past experience. I don't think humans have a great track record. An absolute paradise would be wasted on the world right now."

"Your points are valid ones, Maxine. However, I must leave soon and I will not repeat this offer. You need to decide what you feel comfortable with, but you only have about five minutes to do so. I know it's a difficult decision and a heavy burden to place on one so young. Please try not to feel pressured." Alethea inclined her head at Maxine and waited for her to decide.

Maxine sat on the ground and closed her eyes. She remained that way for the entire five minutes, thinking about her own life and the lives that her decision would affect forever. She pondered whether humanity would squander utopia and if sacrificing her life would be worth the risk. At the end of the five minutes, she took a deep breath and opened her eyes. She rose and walked to stand before Alethea with her head held high.

"I have made my decision."

THANK YOU!

Thank you so much for supporting my work and reading this book. I truly hope you enjoyed reading it as much as I did writing it.

If you liked the book, please consider leaving a review.

Just a few lines would be great. Reviews are not only the highest compliment you can pay to an author, they also help other readers discover and make more informed choices about purchasing books in a crowded online space. Thank you so much in advance.

If you didn't like the book or have concerns,
please email me directly at
heather@heathersilvio.com

ABOUT THE AUTHOR

Heather has written fiction and nonfiction; she is also an actress and licensed psychologist. When she isn't working, she channels her inner flapper as a 1920s jazz and blues singer. She lives in Florida with her wonderful husband Sidney.

Visit https://www.heathersilvio.com for more information and to sign up for her Theatrical Thursdays Newsletter